THE DEAL

TIMOTHY SHARER

www.dizzyemupublishing.com

DIZZY EMU PUBLISHING
1714 N McCadden Place, Hollywood, Los Angeles 90028
www.dizzyemupublishing.com

The Real Deal
Timothy Sharer

ISBN: 9781704918129

First published in the United States
in 2019 by Dizzy Emu Publishing

Copyright © 2019 by Timothy Sharer

Timothy Sharer has asserted his right under the Copyright, Designs and Patents Act 1988 to be identified as the author of this work.

This book is sold subject to the condition that it shall not, by way of trade or otherwise, be lent, resold, hired out, or otherwise circulated without the publisher's prior consent in any form of binding or cover other than that in which it is published and without a similar condition, including this condition, being imposed on the subsequent purchaser.

www.dizzyemupublishing.com

THE REAL DEAL

TIMOTHY SHARER

FADE IN:

EXT. LOS ANGELES - RUNDOWN NEIGHBORHOOD - MORNING

May 2008. Five black teenage bangers wearing their colors are swaggering down the sidewalk. A wino comes staggering along from the opposite direction. As he passes, one of the youths grabs a bottle out of the wino's hand and smashes it against the side of a building.

                    BANGER #1
          Didn't you know that stuff is bad
          for you?

                    THE GANG
              (laughter)
          They walk on a little further
          approaching a prostitute on a corner.

                    PROSTITUTE
              (sarcastically)
          You boys better hurry up and get to
          school. You wouldn't want to be late
          for your thermo dynamics class.

                    BANGER #2
          Shut up ho' and get back to work!

They walk on towards their destination, Jefferson High School, shown in the foreground.

EXT. JEFFERSON HIGH SCHOOL - LAST DAY OF SCHOOL YEAR

Very loud and angry rap music is blasting in the background. A 10-foot barbed wire fence surrounds the school. Pimps and pushers are all around offering the students their services for before and after school partying. Off to the left there is a convertible with guys openly smoking a joint. Over to the right, a young kid is getting rolled for his lunch money.

A well-dressed man sporting a myriad of sparkling gold jewelry walks up to the gang right before they walk into the gate. A conversation takes place, money and drugs are exchanged, then the boys walk into the school yard.

INT. SCHOOL

RONNIE PIPPEN walks down the middle of a noisy crowded hallway filled with teachers trying to get students to class with the students being very uncooperative. A very large student, BIG DADDY, walks up behind Ronnie and gives him a great big bear hug picking him up completely off the ground.

                    RONNIE
            (wheezing still in a
            bear hug)
     What's up Big Daddy?

                    BIG DADDY
            (releasing his grip)
     What's up Pip?...How'd you know it
     was me man?

                    RONNIE
     How could I not know it was you?

                    BIG DADDY
     What are you doing on this end of
     the hall anyway? Don't you have
     trigometry first period?

                    RONNIE
     It's trigonometry but I've got an A
     in the class, so I don't have to
     take the final.

                    BIG DADDY
            (disgusted)
     Is there any class you didn't make
     an A in Einstein?

                    RONNIE
     No, but if you had a grandmother
     like mine, you'd be making A's too.

                    BIG DADDY
     I know that's right.

                    RONNIE
     Coach Thompson asked me to come by
     and talk to him this morning so I
     gotta get.

                    BIG DADDY
            (hand slapping)
     All right man...I guess I'll see you
     tonight around 7. Its pot roast night
     isn't it? Tell granny to fix me a
     plate.

INT. COACHES OFFICE

COACH CECIL THOMPSON, a 71 year old well built black male, is sitting at his desk reading a stack of papers.

KNOCK on the door.

COACH THOMPSON
Come in.

RONNIE
(Entering)
Hey Coach.

COACH THOMPSON
Ronnie! Clear off some of that junk and have a seat...I talked to your grandmother last night. She tells me you are going to be attending Rocksville Community College this fall.

RONNIE
Yes sir.

COACH THOMPSON
Ronnie, you know you don't belong there. You are better than that. You need to get away from here. Heck, they don't even have a football team.

RONNIE
Listen coach, I know what you are saying but I made a promise to my grandmother that I would always take care of her. I can't leave her by herself.

COACH THOMPSON
Ronnie your grandmother is a strong woman. Lord knows she has seen her fair share of trouble since your mother died. You would do her more good getting a degree from a major university or playing football in the pros.

RONNIE
(halfway laughing)
Yea coach, I didn't get even one scholarship offer to play football in college, but I am going to make it in the NFL.

COACH THOMPSON
You know good and well why you didn't get an offer. You played for a low-level school nobody has heard of with teammates that are more concerned with where the party is after the game than with the game itself and
(MORE)

COACH THOMPSON (CONT'D)
for a coach that has failed miserably trying to change it all.

RONNIE
Listen coach...

COACH THOMPSON
(interrupting and forceful)
No, you listen Ronnie Pippen! You are undeniably the best athlete I have coached in my 40 years. You have the hands, the speed and most importantly the smarts to play pro ball and if you think I will just stand on the sidelines and watch you waste that kind of God given talent than you are miserably mistaken my friend.
(settling down)
Ronnie do you know who Coach Buddy Westfield is?

RONNIE
The head coach for Northern California. Yea, sure.

COACH THOMPSON
Well Buddy played for me when I coached out in LA years ago. I called him this morning and he said he would allow you to try out for his team this year with the opportunity for a scholarship for next year if you make it.

RONNIE
But coach...

COACH THOMPSON
Hear me out Ronnie. I know you cannot afford to go to Northern California without working so Buddy said he would arrange for you to have a job on campus. I know it will be difficult being a full-time student, working, and playing football but Ronnie I know you have what it takes.

RONNIE
Coach I appreciate all of this, I really do, but like I said before, I made a promise to my grandmother
(MORE)

                    RONNIE (CONT'D)
          that I would take care of her and be
          there for her.

                    COACH THOMPSON
          I have already talked with her Ronnie.
          You have her complete blessing ...You
          know if she needs anything, she can
          always call me or Big Daddy.
               (stands up)
          Now get on to class. I don't want to
          be the reason you get detention on
          the last day of school.

Ronnie gets up and walks over to coach and embraces him.

                    COACH THOMPSON (CONT'D)
          Remember he is only letting you try
          out as a favor to me. I'm just getting
          you in the door. You are going to
          have to prove yourself once you get
          inside. You are the real deal Ronnie.
          Don't you ever forget that.

Ronnie closes his eyes and squeezes his hug.

                    RONNIE
               (Whispering)
          Thanks Coach.

EXT. PALO ALTO - LAKESIDE HIGH SCHOOL - MORNING

A panning shot of the parking lot of this preppie private
school reveals a vast array of all types of high-priced
automobiles and their cutesy license plates. On the east
side of the parking lot a Viper whips in and stops. On the
west side a Corvette enters and does the same. The two drivers
glare at each other and then smile. The camera pans back to
disclose what the smile is about. A lone unoccupied parking
space is positioned on the front row and distanced equally
between the two vehicles. Both take off at high speed toward
their common destination. The Corvette reaches the spot just
seconds before the Viper then locks up his brakes and slides
perfectly into the open area. The Viper locks up just as it
passes the space.

                    TROY
               (getting out of the
                corvette)
          Hey Bobby, I'm teaching a driver's
          training class after school today.
          Tuition is half price for incurable
          losers. Do you want to be my first
          student?

Bobby starts to say something, stops himself and then shakes his head rolling up his window and screeching off. Troy walks around the back of his car and opens the door on the other side. Inside fuming is his girlfriend MICHELLE STANSBURY.

                    MICHELLE
            (yelling)
How dare you! How dare you! How dare you put my life at risk for a silly parking space.

                    TROY
            (helping her out of
             the car)
Chill out Michelle. Your life was not at risk.

                    MICHELLE
You can't be serious! I can see the headlines now. Prom queen goes sailing through windshield resulting in a tragic and untimely death on the last day of school because of a deranged dim-witted imbecile who thinks he is Flash Gordon.

                    TROY
Flash Gordon?
Do you mean Jeff Gordon?

                    MICHELLE
Sorry...I'm not into NASDAQ racing.

                    TROY
NASDAQ? How about NASCAR?

                    MICHELLE
Whatever, jerk.

                    TROY
Jerk? What has gotten into you?

                    MICHELLE
I'm sorry Troy. I guess I'm just freaked about you going off to Northern Cal. I'm afraid some gorgeous rich chick is going to steal you away.

                    TROY
Don't worry babe. I already have a gorgeous rich chick.
            (smooch on the lips)
Of course, you never can have too many gorgeous rich chicks.

                    MICHELLE
               (walking hurriedly
               away)
          Urghh!! You're disgusting.

                    TROY
               (yelling after her)
          I'm just kidding!

INT. GRANDMA'S HOUSE - EVENING

GRANDMA, a spry 70-year-old, is rocking in her old beat up rocking chair watching a baseball game on an antiquated RCA television. Scattered black and white family photos adorn the wall. The door opens and Ronnie enters. Grandma immediately gets up and they embrace.

                    GRANDMA
          I am so happy for you sugar. Every
          night since you were 10 years old I
          have prayed that God would give you
          a chance to get out of here and make
          something big out of your life and
          now He has.

                    RONNIE
          Are you gonna be okay without me
          grandma?

                    GRANDMA
          If you can keep Dwight away from me
          I think I will be just fine.

                    RONNIE
          Oh, grandma you know Big Daddy loves
          you.

                    GRANDMA
          He loves my cooking.

                    RONNIE
               (walking over to sit
               down)
          Everyone loves your cooking.
               (sniffing)
Is that pot roast?

                    GRANDMA
          It will be ready in thirty minutes.

Ronnie sits down on a couch that has been kept clean but has seen its better days. Grandma sits back in her rocking chair.

                    RONNIE
          What are you watching?

                    GRANDMA
          The Giants and the Dodgers. Barry
          Bonds just hit number 32. His father
          was your grandfather's favorite player
          you know.

                    RONNIE
          Papaw sure loved his baseball...and
          so do you.

                    GRANDMA
          Oh, you know I love all sports
          ...except for soccer. I tried to
          watch an entire game last night. I
          would rather go to the dentist and
          have my last tooth cleaned, drilled,
          capped, and then pulled than have to
          do that again.

                    RONNIE
               (laughing)
          You are so funny grandma.
               (Looks over at the
                television)
          Whenever I make a little money the
          first thing I am going to buy you is
          a new television. That thing is
          ancient.

                    GRANDMA
          Oh no you are not! Your grandfather
          bought me that for our 20th
          anniversary. That was a huge sacrifice
          for him, had to work double shifts
          for a month so he could surprise me
          with it. No sir, it's here to stay.

KNOCK on the door.

                    GRANDMA (CONT'D)
          Now who could that be?

                    RONNIE
          Oops...I forgot to tell you, Big
          Daddy is eating with us tonight.

                    GRANDMA
          Ronnie!

The door suddenly opens, and Big Daddy comes waltzing in the
house.

                    BIG DADDY
          Ya'll must have not heard me knock.
          Oooweee! Something sure smells good.
          Is that pot roast? I sure stopped by
          at a good time.

                    GRANDMA
               (sarcastically)
          Yes, how fortunate. Would you like
          to eat with us while you're here?

                    BIG DADDY
          Granny you know I'd never turn down
          one of your home cooked meals.

                    GRANDMA
               (sternly)
          Listen here Dwight. I don't live in
          the hills of Beverly, I don't keep a
          jug of rheumatis medicine in the
          cabinet and I don't have a cement
          pond in the backyard. So, feel free
          to call me grandmother, grandma, or
          even maamaw. But if you ever call me
          granny again, you'll have to eat my
          pot roast thru a straw.

                    BIG DADDY
               (not a bit phased)
          Sounds good to me grandma...Let's
          eat I'm starving.

THREE MONTHS LATER

INT. DUNN HOUSE - DINING ROOM - AFTERNOON

CLIFF DUNN, Troy Dunn and Michelle Stansbury are sitting at
a large and elegant dining room table preparing to eat lunch
prior to Troy leaving for Northern California University.
The dining room is immaculate resembling a 4-star restaurant.
REBECCA DUNN strolls out of the kitchen carrying a large
covered silver serving tray. With a big smile on her face
Rebecca places the tray in the middle of the table and with
magnificent flair reveals the food of choice.

                    REBECCA
          Whoola! Chicken and dumplings, pinto
          beans. turnip greens and corn bread.
          By special request from the next
          star quarterback for NCU...TROY "THE
          GUN" DUNN.

Cliff and Rebecca enthusiastically clap for their future
hero son. Michelle sits there with a gag me smile and forces
a golf clap.

TROY
Mom...thanks this is so awesome.
This will be my last meal like this
for a while.

MICHELLE
(chuckling)
It probably will be. Isn't NCU a
white school?

Everyone looks up at Michelle somewhat disgustingly.

MICHELLE (CONT'D)
I'm not trying to be rude...I mean
...come on you have to admit that's
a little weird...I mean Mrs. Dunn
you are a great cook you could have
fixed him anything...

TROY
(interrupting)
This just happens to be my favorite
meal since I was a kid...no big deal.

REBECCA
Michelle...honey...back when Troy
was born, Cliff was still in law
school and could only work part time.
We had very little money and we were
taken in by an elderly black couple
from the church. They helped us in
many ways, one is the art of southern
cooking.

CLIFF
Just try it...You'll be hooked.

MICHELLE
I don't think so.

REBECCA
(walking back to the
kitchen)
Don't worry...I have a salad and a
chicken sandwich in the kitchen for
you.

TROY
Ok...Ok...let's just eat please. Dad
would you say grace.

Rebecca hurries back from the kitchen, serves Michelle, then
everyone holds hands around the table.

                    CLIFF
          Thank you God for the food we have
          before us and thank you again for
          bringing us together as a family.
          Watch over Troy as he goes off to
          college and help him to make wise
          decisions as he begins this journey.
          Amen.

They all begin to eat.

                    REBECCA
          Are you sure you don't want us to go
          up and help you move in?

                    TROY
          No mom. I'll be all right. I don't
          have a lot of decorating to do. Just
          a few Jennifer Aniston posters to
          pin up, and then I'm done.

                    MICHELLE
          And they'll be coming down on my
          first visit.

                    REBECCA
          Have you talked with your roommate
          yet?

                    TROY
          Actually, Coach Westfield told me he
          was going to try and get me a room
          by myself. So as of right now I'm
          flying solo.

                    MICHELLE
          Do you want to be by yourself?

                    TROY
          No doubt...that would be a huge bonus.

                    CLIFF
          The dorms are relatively small out
          there and guys, especially in football
          dorms, can be pretty gross.

                    MICHELLE
          Yes, but if you have a roommate from
          another part of the country you might
          learn something new.

                    CLIFF
          Yea...my roommate was from Texas. I
          learned that it is actually possible
                         (MORE)

                        CLIFF (CONT'D)
                  to light a fart...and that if you
                  place someone's fingertips instead
                  of their whole hand in warm water
                  while they sleep, they will pee their
                  bed quicker.

                              TROY
                        (laughter)

                              REBECCA
                        (smiling, shaking her
                        head)
                  That's my Cliff.

                              MICHELLE
                  Now I know where Troy gets it from.
                  Like father like son.

                              TROY
                        (high fiving his dad) You got that
                  right!

INT. GRANDMA'S HOUSE - AFTERNOON

Ronnie, Grandma and Big Daddy all teary-eyed standing in the
den area with a very large old packed suitcase in view sitting
by the door.

                              GRANDMA
                  Now you're sure you got your bus
                  ticket?

                              RONNIE
                        (patting chest pocket)
                  Yes Grandma.

                              GRANDMA
                  You have the bag of snacks I made
                  you for the trip?

                              RONNIE
                  What bag?

                              BIG DADDY
                  Oh...my bad. I didn't know they were
                  for Ronnie's trip...I have a bag of
                  Reece's Pieces in my car if you want
                  me to go get them.

                              RONNIE
                  That's okay man. I don't need to be
                  eating junk right before football
                  starts.

HORN HONKS

                    RONNIE (CONT'D)
               I guess that's my cab.

Grandma walks over and hugs Ronnie.

                    GRANDMA
                 (still embracing)
               Your mom would be so proud of you.
               You turned out to be such a good
               kid. When you walk out that door,
               you will take your first step of
               manhood. Never forget that first
               step, and never forget where you
               came from and what I have tried to
               teach you.

                    RONNIE
                 (tearing up)
               I am what I am because of you and I
               will never forget that.

HORN HONKS

                    RONNIE (CONT'D)
               I need to get.

Walks over to Big Daddy, shakes his hand, and then turns it into a hug.

                    RONNIE (CONT'D)
               I'm gonna miss you my friend.

                    BIG DADDY
               Don't worry. I'll find a way to come
               visit you.

They all walk out on the porch. Grandma and Big Daddy stop. Ronnie keeps walking to the taxi and throws his suitcase into the trunk.

                    CAB DRIVER
               Where you headin'?

                    RONNIE
               Bus station.

                    CAB DRIVER
               You got it chief.

Ronnie opens the back door to get in but before he sits in the cab, he turns around for one final wave.

                    BIG DADDY
               (reaches over and
               puts his arm around
               grandma)
          Don't you be worrying about grandma
          ...I'll be taking good care of her.

Grandma grimaces. Ronnie gets in the cab and it drives away.

EXT. DUNN HOUSE - AFTERNOON

The Dunn home, perched high on a small hill, has lushly
landscaped front and back yards. A grove of oak trees growing
behind the home creates an emerald green background image.

The stonework in the double driveway circling around the
front of the home gives it a luxurious look. The two pillars
adorning the front entrance of the home creates a colonial-
style architecture. The whitewashed brick on the home produces
a slight mirror image, with a modern twist, of Scarlett
O'Hara's home in *Gone With The Wind*. The Dunn family and
Michelle are standing by Troy's corvette which has a U-Haul
trailer attached to it.

                    MICHELLE
          This is the most uncool thing I have
          ever seen. I hope nobody recognizes
          you.

                    TROY
          I'm gonna miss you too Michelle.

                    MICHELLE
          I'm sorry...I'm just trying to protect
          your image. You know I'm going to
          miss you. It's just that you should
          have hired somebody to get your things
          up there or something.

                    REBECCA
          Honey are you sure you don't want us
          to follow you up there and help you
          unload.

                    TROY
               (grinning)
          Yea mom...won't you and dad do that.

                    CLIFF
               (sarcastically)
          Sure thing son...just go on ahead.
          We'll be right behind you.

                              TROY
                    No mom...I'm sure there'll be someone
                    from the football office to help me.

                              REBECCA
                    Well be sure and call me as soon as
                    you get there.

                              TROY
                    Mom, it's only a two-hour drive and...

Dad gives him the "you better listen to your mama" look.

                              TROY (CONT'D)
                    Okay. You're right. I'll call you
                    when I get there.

Walks over to dad and they embrace.

                              CLIFF
                    See you on TV superstar.

                              TROY
                    I love you dad.

Reaches over and hugs mom and gives her a kiss on the cheek.

                              TROY (CONT'D)
                    I love you mom.

                              REBECCA
                        (crying)
                    You be good son, and don't forget to
                    call me.

Turns around to Michelle hugs her, then kisses her on the lips.

                              TROY
                    I'll call you tonight when I get
                    settled in.

                              MICHELLE
                    You better...I'll try and come visit
                    as soon as I can.

They kiss again. He gets in the car, waves, and drives off with the trailer clanking as he goes on down the road.

                              MICHELLE (CONT'D)
                        (under her breath)
                    Gosh...I hope none of my friends see
                    him.

INT. DORM ADMINISTRATION BUILDING - LATE AFTERNOON

The registration area is a large room decorated with many colorful signs, balloons, and miscellaneous paraphernalia welcoming arrivals for the new semester. There is a table set up manned with three hotties coordinating room assignments, class and practice schedules, and book requirements. The signs of A-L, M-R, and S-Z are posted on the table with a line of big (predominately) white athletes waiting in line. Troy is standing second in line with a travel bag strapped over each shoulder. The student in front of Troy finishes his paperwork and moves to the left. Troy walks up to the table.

                    HOTTIE
          Hey cutie what's your name?

                    TROY
          Troy Dunn.

                    HOTTIE
          That's Dunn with a D?

                    TROY
         Uh...yea...Dunn with a D.

                    HOTTIE
         Well the only reason I even bring it
         up is...well do you see those little
         sign thingies in front of the table
         there?

Troy looks down and sees he is standing in the M-R line.

                    TROY
         Oops.

                    HOTTIE
         Uh...yea...Well not to worry. I'm a
         trained professional.

She reaches over to the box in the station next to her. The girl working that station looks at her questioning.

                    HOTTIE (CONT'D)
         Excuse the reach but I have a code
         red.

The girl immediately looks up at Troy and smiles. Troy just shrugs his shoulders.

                    HOTTIE (CONT'D)
            (flipping through the
            files)
         Okay lets see...Dunn...Troy Dunn.

                              TROY
                    That would be me.

                              HOTTIE
                    Okay Troy...in this packet you have
                    your practice schedule, class
                    schedule, required textbook list
                    ...pick them up at the bookstore
                    tonight...and your room assignment.
                    Let's see...you are in Moody hall in
                    room 207.
                         (looks over papers)
                    Wow...you must know somebody in high
                    places. Looks like, as of right now,
                    you have the room to yourself.

                              TROY
                         (Excitedly)
                    Yes!

                              HOTTIE
                    Well here's your packet and I guess
                    I'll see you around.

                              TROY
                    Yea thanks.

Troy grabs his packet, gathers his travel bags and exits.

INT. DORM ROOM

Door opens and Troy walks in loaded down with his belongings.

                              TROY
                         (looking around)
                    Small...but it will work.

KNOCK on the door.

Before Troy can answer, the door flies open and LOUIS REYNOLDS
a black center from Seattle, PAUL HAMPTON a white defensive
lineman from Houston and WILLIE CUNNINGHAM a black linebacker
from San Diego, come blasting in.

                              LOUIS
                    We would have baked you some cookies
                    but I lost great-grandma's recipe.
                    What's up?...I'm Louis Reynolds.
                         (Holds out his hand))

                              PAUL
                         (holds out his hand)
                    Paul Hampton...Houston, Texas.

                    WILLIE
              (holds out his hand)
         Willie Cunningham...what's up man?

                    TROY
              (shaking hands)
         What's up fellas?...I'm Troy Dunn.

                    LOUIS
         Oh...so you're the hotshot quarterback
         from that private school in Palo
         Alto, Troy the Gun Dunn. Well I hope
         you are as good as people say...our
         quarterbacks last year, well lets
         just say there was a lot of room for
         improvement.

                    TROY
         I'm going to do my best to get that
         changed. Where you guys from?

                    PAUL
         You know Troy you should never ask
         where someone is from?

                    TROY
         Why is that?

                    PAUL
         Because if they were from Texas,
         they would have already told you.
         And if they're not, then it really
         doesn't matter.

Louis and Willie shake their heads and roll their eyes.

                    TROY
              (laughing)
         Yea...I heard about you Texas boys.

                    WILLIE
         Do you need a hand getting your stuff?

                    TROY
         Sure man that would be great.

                    WILLIE
              (Texas accent)
         Paul why don't you round up a posse
         and help Troy get his gear in his
         room. Me and my compadre here are
         going to mosey on down to the
         bookstore to get some needed supplies
         for our first day of education
         tomorrow.

Throws up the deuce.

                    WILLIE (CONT'D)
          See ya.

Willie and Louis leave the room.

                    PAUL
          Well let's get you moved in and then
          you can take me to get some dinner.

                    TROY
          You got it.

EXT. DORM ADMINISTRATION AREA - EVENING

A taxicab pulls up in front of the building. Ronnie gets out of the back seat as the trunk of the cab opens up. He grabs out his suitcase, pays the driver, and moves as fast as the suitcase allows towards the entrance of the building.

He pushes on the door to find it locked. He sees a sign posted on the other door stating "Use side entrance after 9:00 pm". He hurriedly races around the side of the building and bursts open the side entrance door. He plods up a flight of steps and opens another door. He sees a female student walking across the foyer and rushes over to her.

                    RONNIE
             (out of breath)
          Excuse me...excuse me Miss.

                    STUDENT
             (Standoffish)
          Yes?

                    RONNIE
          Could you please tell me where the
          dorm registration table is?

                    STUDENT
          Are you a football player?

                    RONNIE
          I hope to be.

                    STUDENT
             (pointing to her left)
          The football team registers down
          that hallway, but you better hurry,
          registration ended 15 minutes ago.

                    RONNIE
          Thanks.

Ronnie picks up his suitcase and rushes down the hallway.

INT. DORM ADMINISTRATION AREA - EVENING

One lone 40-year-old female staffer, SHARON HIGBEE, is at the registration table boxing up various items. All the signs and paraphernalia have been taken down. Ronnie briskly walks over to the table and drops his suitcase.

                   SHARON
          Can I help you?

                   RONNIE
          Yes, please. My name is Ronnie Pippen.
          I'm checking in.

                   SHARON
         Are you a football player?

                   RONNIE
         Yes ma'am.

                   SHARON
           (smiling)
          I appreciate the courtesy, but that
          ma'am stuff sure makes me feel old.

                   RONNIE
          Sorry...just the way I was raised.

                   SHARON
         To respect your elders?

                   RONNIE
         To respect people in a position that
          can help me out when I'm in a bind.
          I know I'm late, I know registration
          is over, and I know the only thing
          that is keeping me from having to
          sleep on that couch over there is
          your kindness.

                   SHARON
           (smiling)
          Yes you are late and yes if I wanted
          to be a jerk you would be on that
          couch tonight...What happened anyway?
          Did your car breakdown?

                   RONNIE
          I wish I had a car to break down.
          No, I took a bus from LA and we had
          a flat tire. We were on the side of
          the road for over three hours.

SHARON
Yuk...ok what was your last name again?

RONNIE
Pippen.

SHARON
(looking in a nearly
empty registration
box)
As in Gladys Knight and the...never mind too young. Okay Ronnie Pippen. Let's see...here is your class and practice schedule. Here is your required book list. The bookstore is closed so you will have to get them after class tomorrow. I see Coach Westfield has set you up with a job. You'll need to be at the cafeteria in the morning by 6:15. Looks like you'll be working the serving line.

RONNIE
Hey. A job is a job. You do what you gotta do.

SHARON
I like your attitude Ronnie Pippen. Let me see here...uh...looks like they didn't assign you to a room. Clerical error I'm sure. But no problem we can do that right now.
(she picks up a folder
and scans over it)
Let's see if there is any room on the second floor. Upper classmen get first dibs on the first floor. Yea here we go. Room 207 needs a roommate. Here is your key. Just go out the same way you came in and then turn to the left. It will be the first building on your right. Go through the first set of glass doors and up the stairway. Then just look for room 207 about halfway down the hallway.

RONNIE
That'll work. Thanks again for helping me out.

Ronnie picks up his suitcase and starts heading to his dorm.

                    SHARON
          Don't forget to be at work by 6:15.

INT. DORM ROOM

Room 207 has been completely decked out with Troy's things.
A television and complete sound system are stationed against
the front wall resting on a table that separates the two
desks which are against the side walls. A fully stocked
miniature refrigerator is on the floor underneath. The shelves
over the desk on the left have been filled with the textbooks
purchased earlier today. The shelves over the desk on the
right has miscellaneous pictures of Troy with family and
friends. The left bunk has various bags resting on it, and
the right bunk has a wide array of clothes stacked randomly
on it. Troy is sitting in a low backed chair talking on the
telephone.

                    TROY
               (phone)
          I met some guys on the team. They're
          real cool. Some dude from Texas helped
          me move in so I took him to eat some
          wings. Yea, the room looks fine. A
          little small but...

CLINKING of the door lock.

The door opens and Ronnie is standing there, suitcase beside
him, pulling his key out of the lock.

                    TROY (CONT'D)
               (phone)
          Hold on a sec mom.
               (muffs hand over phone)
          Can I help you?

                    RONNIE
          Uh...yea...is this room 207?

                    TROY
          Sure is.

                    RONNIE
               (holding out his hand)
          I'm Ronnie Pippen. I guess we're
          gonna be roommates.

                    TROY
               (disappointedly shaking
                his hand)
          Are you sure you are in room 207?

                    REBECCA (VO)
          Who is it hun?

                    RONNIE
          We'll here's the key for it. What's
          the matter? You don't like me already?

                    REBECCA (V.O.)
          What did he just say?

                    TROY
              (phone)
          Mom I need to call you back...no
          it's ok...I'll call you back. Goodbye.

Troy hangs up the phone, turns around, and faces Ronnie.

                    TROY (CONT'D)
          Sorry man. I just thought I had the
          room to myself. I'm Troy Dunn. What
          was your name again?

                    RONNIE
          Ronnie Pippen.

                    TROY
          Where you from?

                    RONNIE
          L.A. Yourself?

                    TROY
          The Palo Alto area.
              (looking around the
               room)
          Aw man...I kind of taken over the
          place. Let's go out to your car and
          I'll help you get your stuff in,
          then I'll get my junk out of your
          way.

                    RONNIE
          What you see is what you get man.
          I'm a very light traveler.

                    TROY
              (turning around towards
               the refrigerator)
          That's cool. Want something to drink?

                    RONNIE
          No man...thanks...but I don't drink.

Troy opens the refrigerator and it is wall to wall with Ozarka
water bottles. He reaches in and gets two bottles out.

                    TROY
          Sorry man but I insist. I don't ever
          drink alone.

Ronnie, smiling, takes the bottle reads the label and tries
to hide his amusement.

                    TROY (CONT'D)
          What's so funny?

                    RONNIE
              (trying to conceal
               his smile)
          Nothing man.

                    TROY
          No really what is so funny.

                    RONNIE
          Sorry but I just think it's funny
          that people buy what they can get
          out of their next door neighbor's
          water hose for free.

                    TROY
          It's not the same water. Bottled
          water is better for you. It is
          purified.

                    RONNIE
              (Takes a swig)
          Sure it is.

Ronnie reaches up with his right hand and grabs a hand full
of air and then does the same with his left. He then cups
his hands together and shakes them around.

                    RONNIE (CONT'D)
          I'll sell you a batch of freshly
          mixed purified air made only with
          the finest ingredients.

Ronnie then presses together the tips of his index finger
and thumb on both hands forming a circle and puts them over
his eyes.

                    RONNIE (CONT'D)
          Or how about special glasses that
          let you...
              (looking side to side)
          see things that are around you.

                        TROY
              Okay...okay...you made your point. I
              can see we are going to get along
              just fine.

Troy hurriedly starts throwing his stuff from Ronnie's side
to his side of the room.

                        TROY (CONT'D)
              Which side of the closet do you want?

                        RONNIE
              Makes no difference.

                        TROY
              Okay...I'll take the left. I already
              have some stuff hanging.

Ronnie hangs his clothes up and starts setting up his side
of the room.

                        TROY (CONT'D)
              So, what position do you play?

                        RONNIE
              I played a little corner but mostly
              at receiver.

                        TROY
              Cool...I'm a quarterback. We'll be
              working out together...You know I
              just cannot wait for practice tomorrow
              afternoon. Some people are addicted
              to drugs some to alcohol. Me...I'll
              be the first to admit, I'm addicted
              to playing football. When I was eight
              years old, my dad took me to my first
              professional football game. I can
              still remember Jerry Rice jukeing
              some poor defensive back...
                  (awkwardly shows a
                   move)
              so bad that the db crossed up his
              own feet and fell flat on his face.
              All Young had to do was float the
              ball out there and let Rice run under
              it for a sixty-yard touchdown. That
              was pure poetry my friend. Ever since
              that day, I knew that's what I wanted
              to do.

26.

RONNIE
(laughing)
I don't think you're dream of jukeing out a defensive back is going to come true anytime soon.

TROY
You know what I mean man. My dream is to play in the NFL. What about yourself? What do you dream about?

RONNIE
I don't do much dreaming. I'm too busy dealing with reality.

TROY
Come on man. It can't be that bad. Do you remember the first football game your dad took you to?

RONNIE
My father never took me to a football game. I never really knew him. He left me and my mother when I was three. All I can remember is my mother crying a lot. We moved to LA and stayed with my grandmother.

TROY
How long was that your home?

RONNIE
From then to about...
(looks at his watch)
...five minutes ago.

TROY
Does your mother still live there?

RONNIE
My mother died two years ago of cancer.

TROY
I'm sorry man.

RONNIE
It's okay ...you know I probably spent more time with her in the years we had together than most people do with their mothers in a lifetime.

TROY
Why is that?
(MORE)

TROY (CONT'D)
I have spent a lot of time with my mom, but I can't say we really hung out together. I guess I had too many friends.

RONNIE
I had plenty of friends but not too many I would hang out with. Being without a father figure in my life my mother and grandmother taught me right from wrong at an early age and instilled in me the importance of getting a good education. Where I grew up there was a lot of wrong and studying was seen as a waste of time. You could make more money on the streets hustling than you could with a high school diploma. So, I spent most of my free time working out or at home.

TROY
I guess it can be that bad. Man, I live a sheltered life.

RONNIE
You know what they say, if it doesn't kill you it will make you stronger.

TROY
If that's true you should be Hulk Hogan.

RONNIE
How about The Rock.

TROY
Because he's black?

RONNIE
(joking)
Because he is better looking! Why is everything so racial?

TROY
Okay...I see how it's going to be.

Ronnie falls back on his bunk.

RONNIE
It's your turn. Tell me your life story. Which side of the hood are you claiming?

Troy continues setting up his side of the room.

                    TROY
          Like I said, I grew up pretty
          sheltered from the crap you were
          exposed to. My dad is a partner in a
          big law firm in San Francisco. He
          makes a lot of money, so I have lived
          a pretty easy life. Even though he
          is working a lot, he has always been
          there for me...never missed a football
          game from peewees through high school.

                    RONNIE
          I guess our backgrounds are really
          not that different...except for
          everything! So, what's up with your
          mother? I guess you better call her
          back to let her know that I don't
          have you tied up in the closet.

                    TROY
          Sorry man she just gets nervous
          easily...After I was born my mom
          never worked outside the home. She
          met my dad in college, and they got
          married right after he graduated.
          They had me while he was still in
          law school. I think she had a year
          or two left before she would graduate,
          but she never went back. My dad always
          joked she got what she wanted, an
          MRS degree so there was no need to
          go back.

                    RONNIE
             (smiling)
          Do you have a girlfriend? Or
          girlfriends? Or boyfriend for that
          matter?

                    TROY
          Easy...I have a girlfriend, singular.
          We have dated for a little over a
          year.

                    RONNIE
          Are ya'll serious?

                    TROY
          I don't know. I think she might be.
          Sometimes it just doesn't feel right.
          My parents don't care too much for
          her but who knows.
                    (MORE)

                    TROY (CONT'D)
                (looking around the
                room)
            I think we got it looking as good as
            its going to get. I've already eaten
            but if you want to go get something
            I'll tag along and kind of show you
            the area.

                    RONNIE
            No, I better get to bed. I've got to
            get up at 5:45.

                    TROY
            My gosh! What time does your first
            class start?

                    RONNIE
            It doesn't start till 10 but I've
            got to be at work by 6:15.

                    TROY
            Are you kidding me? I take it you
            are not on a scholarship.

                    RONNIE
            Actually, I was offered one, but I
            turned it down.

Troy stares at him surprised.

                    RONNIE (CONT'D)
            I told coach to give it to someone a
            little more needy. He said he knew
            some kid from Palo Alto and...
                (smiling)
            naw I'm a last-minute recruit. Coach
            told me I could try and walk on the
            team. Tomorrow's practice will be
            the first time he will have ever
            seen me play.

                    TROY
            Wow...he hasn't even seen any tapes
            of you?

                    RONNIE
            There aren't any. Any that were made
            have either been lost, stolen, or of
            such poor quality that they are of
            no good. My school did not have much
            interest in making quality tapes for
            future use. No one from my district,
            much less from my school, has gone
            on to play for a division 1 college.

                        TROY
            So, when you step on that field for
            the first time, you will be making
            history.

                        RONNIE
            Yea...I guess so. I never really
            thought of it that way.

                        TROY
            What do you mean you guess so? That
            is freaking huge. Something you can
            always be proud of. Tell the grandkids
            and all.

                        RONNIE
            Before I can worry about what I am
            going to tell my grandkids, I have
            to make the team. Not too many walk-
            ons do. I'm gonna need all the help
            I can get.

                        TROY
            I got you bro.

Ronnie reaches over and they fist bump.

                        TROY (CONT'D)
            That's what roommates are for...What
            time do you have to get up again?

                        RONNIE
            At 5:45.

                        TROY
                (facetiously)
            Could you not turn the light on? I
            need my beauty sleep.

Ronnie reaches around and grabs a pillow off the bed and
smacks him.

                        TROY (CONT'D)
        Hey!

INT. CAFETERIA - MORNING

A clock on the wall shows 6:25. There is a line of about 50
students impatiently waiting to go into the serving area.
There is a Spanish lady, ALEJANDRA ORTEGA, standing by a
sliding glass door that is preventing their entrance. TED
WALTERS, a very unlikable type of fellow, is fifth in line
followed by 2 of his equally smart aleck friends.

                              TED
                    C'mon Maria. It's freaking 6:25.
                    They're not going to fire you letting
                    us in five minutes early.

                           ALEJANDRA
                         (in a very thick
                          Spanish accent)
                    No thank you sir. My boss man say
                    let theem en at sex thirty.

                           SMART ALECK #1
                         (in a faked Spanish
                          accent)
                    Maria, it is sex twenty sex. Mucho
                    hungryo. We go in or I call INS.

Everyone within earshot chuckles.

                           ALEJANDRA
                    Sir, me llama Alejandra. No is Maria.
                    Call me by my real name por favor.

                           SMART ALECK #2
                    We'll call you any name we want to
                    Alex Andra!

                           ALEJANDRA
                    No, no. You are getting me confused
                    with Alex Tandra, your boyfreend. He
                    tuld me about jew. He say jew are a
                    good keesser.

The people chuckling earlier are laughing hysterically now.

                           SMART ALECK #2
                         (looking around) What did she say?

                           ALEJANDRA
                         (sliding open the
                          door and smiling)
                    Jew may go in now.

INT. SERVING AREA

The serving line is set up in typical cafeteria fashion.
Trays and utensils first, then a selection of breakfast foods,
and a choice of milk or orange juice at the end. Ronnie is
standing behind the scrambled eggs tray, serving spoon in
hand, sporting a standard white uniform and hair net. The
students start processing down the line.

                              TED
                    Yo lunch lady. Slap me down some of
                    them eggs.

Ronnie gets a spoonful of eggs and splats it messily on his tray.

                    TED (CONT'D)
          Nice try lunch lady but you still
          need a little practice.

                    SMART ALECK #1
          Yea, you and Maria out there need to
          go back to cafeteria school for a
          little refresher course.

The boys start moving down the line.

                    TED
          Oh yea...cute hair net. You better
          get it back to your mama before her
          shift starts.

Laughter from the boys.

                    STUDENT
              (walking behind the
               boys)
          Don't worry about it. They're a bunch
          of punks.

                    RONNIE
          I know...thanks.

INT. BILLINGHAM CLASSROOM - MORNING

The classroom is quite large with about 100 mostly Caucasian students already in their seats. PROFESSOR LLOYD BILLINGHAM is standing at the front behind a podium reviewing his notes. He is dressed very dapper sporting a tie and jacket. Across the blackboard behind him is written in chalk: American History 101. Come To My Class Prepared Or Don't Come At All! Ted and his cohorts are sitting in the back talking amongst themselves.

                    PROFESSOR BILLINGHAM
          Good morning class. I am Professor
          Billingham, and this is American
          History 101. If you are in the wrong
          class, please get up right now and
          go directly to the admissions office
          and let them know you are an idiot
          and do not belong at this institution
          of higher learning.
              (laughter from students)
          I take my job very serious and I
          take American history very seriously.
          If we don't know the history of this
                    (MORE)

32.

PROFESSOR BILLINGHAM (CONT'D)
country and learn from the mistakes
of our founding fathers, and believe
me there were many, we are doomed to
repeat them. I have many rules for
this class which are outlined in the
syllabus that is on your desks. I
expect you to know them and adhere
to them. There are two I want you to
take special note of. Number one
...come to my class on time. I detest
distractions of any sort, so if you
cannot be here on time, I will have
some chairs set up in the hallway,
and you may listen from there. Number
two..
    (turns and points to
    the blackboard)
Come to my class prepared or don't
come at all. I expect assignments to
be read and projects to be completed
on time. There will be no grace,
there will be no second chances. Now
everyone open your textbook and read
pages 5, 6 and 7. We will discuss
these pages in five minutes. Begin.

The students looking somewhat bewildered immediately open
their books and begin reading. Professor Billingham resumes
reviewing his notes. The class is completely silent. Ronnie
opens the door that is located in the rear of the class. He
is still wearing his uniform. He walks in and looks for a
seat in the back. Professor Billingham immediately looks up
with an astonished look upon his face.

                TED
    (whispering)
Oh man, its lunch lady.

          PROFESSOR BILLINGHAM
If I believed in a higher power, I
would be asking what in God's name
has just disrupted my class. But
since I don't, I will just simply
inquire of you, sir, of the reason
you are late and why are you wearing
that ridiculous....
    (stutters looking for
    a word)
thing on the top of your head?

RONNIE
(reaching up and pulling the hair net off)
I...I...I didn't realize I was still wearing it. Sorry sir.

PROFESSOR BILLINGHAM
(mockingly)
Bu...bu...but that still doesn't answer the inquiry about your tardiness. But no matter, since I am a reasonable man, I will assume you just had a hard time deciding on just the right attire to wear on your first day of class.
(classroom laughter)
Now find a seat. We will be discussing pages 5, 6, and 7 in about 1 minute.
(under his breath but loud enough for the class to hear)
I cannot wait for the jewels of wisdom you will be contributing.

Professor Billingham begins reading his notes again. The class continues reading except for Ronnie. A little time passes, and Professor Billingham randomly looks up and does a quick take after he sees Ronnie just sitting in his seat.

PROFESSOR BILLINGHAM (CONT'D)
(catching the eye of Ronnie)
What is your name young man?

RONNIE
Ronnie Pippen.

PROFESSOR BILLINGHAM
Well Ronnie Pippen, what high school did you attend?

RONNIE
Jefferson High...in LA.

PROFESSOR BILLINGHAM
Well are textbooks optional at the prestigious Jefferson High School in LA.

RONNIE
No sir.

PROFESSOR BILLINGHAM
Well then where is yours?

                    RONNIE
          I checked into my dorm late last
          night. The bookstore was already
          closed when I got my class schedule.

                    PROFESSOR BILLINGHAM
          But it was open before class started
          this morning.

                    RONNIE
          I had to be at work at 6:15...came
          straight to class.

                    PROFESSOR BILLINGHAM
          You have an answer for everything,
          don't you boy? I bet you're on the
          football team.

Ronnie just sits in his chair embarrassed and silent.

                    PROFESSOR BILLINGHAM (CONT'D)
          Well, are you?

                    RONNIE
          Yes sir.

                    PROFESSOR BILLINGHAM
          What a surprise. I don't like
          athletics. The only thing it does is
          take money away from academia so
          that a few thousand yahoos have
          something to do besides mow their
          yards on Saturday afternoons.

                    RONNIE
          A few thousand? NCU averaged over 60
          thousand per game last year.

                    PROFESSOR BILLINGHAM
                (angrily cutting him
                 off)
          That's enough! I am not going to
          lower myself by debating a football
          player about the merits or, lack
          thereof, of college athletics. Now I
          don't know the exact average
          attendance of NCU football games,
          but I do know that you are not going
          to prance into my classroom at any
          time you want to, unprepared, and
          with a haughty attitude just because
          you are on the football team. You
          can tell your Coach Buddy Westfield,
          as always, none of his players will
                         (MORE)

                    PROFESSOR BILLINGHAM (CONT'D)
               be receiving any special privileges
               this year. Do you get that Mister
               Pippen?

Ronnie sits unresponsive. Ted and his buddies smile and
chuckle.

                    PROFESSOR BILLINGHAM (CONT'D)
               Now class, let's get back to the
               matter at hand...American History.
               Turn to page 5.

EXT. PRACTICE FIELD-AFTERNOON

The Northern Californian football team is lined up in eleven
rows of ten across the practice field wearing team issued
shorts, sweatshirts, and helmets. There are five captains
standing at the front facing everyone else.

Ten coaches are dispersed amongst the team barking out
motivational phrases to the players as they perform different
stretches and group exercises.

The strength coach is standing at the front with the captains
leading all the stretches and exercises. COACH BUDDY WESTFIELD
is standing in the bird's nest wearing a headset and holding
a blow horn.

                    STRENGTH COACH
                 (blows his whistle)
               Listen up! We need all the O and D
               linemen on the east side 10. All
               quarterbacks, running backs, and
               linebackers on the east side 30.
               Receivers and defensive backs to the
               west side end zone. All kickers and
               punters to the soccer field behind
               us. Let's go! Let's go! Let's go!

All of the players immediately start running to their assigned
areas, followed by the coaches.

EXT. WEST SIDE END ZONE-AFTERNOON

The receivers and defensive backs are standing in two single
file lines on the goal line. Two coaches are standing on the
40-yard line with stop watches in hand. There is an assistant
with a clip board hovering around them both.

                    COACH GRIFFIN
               Okay guys you all know the drill. At
               the sound of the whistle take off
               and run through the 40.
                         (MORE)

                    COACH GRIFFIN (CONT'D)
               (pause)
          Hey Spence, you had the fastest 40
          time last year right?

                    SPENCE
          You know it coach. It was a four
          three five, but I think you had a
          slow trigger finger. Shoulda been a
          four two five.
               (laughter from players)

                    COACH GRIFFIN
          Well lightening, why don't you start
          this show off. Joffrey run with him.

                    JOFFREY
               (sarcastically)
          Thanks a lot coach.

Spence and Joffrey walk over to the goal line loosening up
their legs as they go. They get set and the whistle blows.
They both get good starts, but Spence puts it in another
gear the last 20 yards. The two coaches snap their stop
watches as Spence and Joffrey cross the forty.

                    COACH #2
          Joffrey Walker four point eight.

                    ASSISTANT
          Got it coach.

                    COACH GRIFFIN
               (smiling)
          Spence Mathis four two five.

The assistant coach smiles and writes down the time.

                    COACH GRIFFIN (CONT'D)
               (loudly)
          Four two five. Good job Mr. Mathis.

Joffrey high fives Spence as they jog back towards the end
zone. The other players yell out various "atta boys" to Spence
as they prepare to get timed as well. The next pair of runners
take off and the camera pans back to see Ronnie standing
last in line wearing a pair of shoes that looks like he just
took them out of the garbage. The player he is paired with
to run, JERMAINE, is looking at the shoes with a rather
confused look on his face.

                    JERMAINE
          Yo homey. What the heck do you have
          on your feet?

                    RONNIE
              (looking down)
          Uh...shoes?

                    JERMAINE
          I know they're shoes but they look
          like you got them out of the dumpster
          behind Goodwill. Man, if you need
          any duct tape to keep that heel on
          just let me know.

                    RONNIE
          Hey man why don't you just worry
          about what you are going to say to
          the coaches after I smoke you in
          these Goodwill dumpster shoes.

                    JERMAINE
          Chill out man. I'm just bustin' on
          you. They didn't give you any shoes
          when you got your equipment?

                    RONNIE
          Nope. The equipment manager said he
          would issue shoes when and if I made
          the team. Something about he's afraid
          if I got cut, that's the last he
          would see of 'em.

                    JERMAINE
          Man...walk-ons get no respect.

The two walk up to the goal line and wait for the whistle to
blow.

                    COACH WESTFIELD
              (on headset)
          How's it going down there?

                    COACH #1 (VO)
          We just have two more to run. Everyone
          looks like they're about at the same
          speed they were at when they left
          for the summer. Of course, Spence
          had the fastest time with a four two
          five.

                    COACH WESTFIELD
          Four two five? I'm licking my chops
          coach.

The whistle blows and the runners take off. Ronnie leads
from start to finish. After they cross the finish line
Jermaine jogs over to Ronnie.

JERMAINE
(somewhat out of breath)
Man...Goodwill. You got some wheels.

COACH #2
Jermaine Perkins...four five five.

COACH GRIFFIN
(looking at his watch)
What's this kid's name?

ASSISTANT
(reading off his clip
board)
Ronnie Piper. What did he run?

COACH GRIFFIN
Four thr…
(yelling)
Mr. Piper come over here please.

Ronnie jogs over to the coach.

RONNIE
Yes sir.

COACH GRIFFIN
Where did you play ball at and what in heaven's name do you have on your feet?

RONNIE
Jefferson High School in LA and the best football shoes I own.

COACH GRIFFIN
Didn't Bucky get you a pair of turf Nikes?

RONNIE
The equipment manager? Naw. He was afraid I was gonna steal 'em or something.

Coach Griffin shakes his head in disgust.

COACH GRIFFIN
(yelling)
Buckeeeeeee!

BUCKY
(running over)
Yes coach.

                    COACH GRIFFIN
          Would you please get this young man
          a pair of fricking turf shoes?

                    BUCKY
          Yes sir.
               (Turns to Ronnie)
          What size?

                    RONNIE
          Twelve and a half.

                    COACH #1
          Be sure and have him finger printed
          before you give them to him.

                    BUCKY
               (Looking confused)
          Sir?

                    COACH GRIFFIN
               (loudly)
          Never mind. Just hurry!

                    BUCKY
          Yes sir.

Bucky runs off towards the locker room.

                    COACH GRIFFIN
          Ronnie go back down there and run it
          again. This time with some decent
          shoes.

                    RONNIE
          Yes coach.

Ronnie turns and jogs off.

                    COACH GRIFFIN
               (over headset)
          Coach Westfield. I think you better
          come down and see this.

                    COACH WESTFIELD(VO)
          Good news or bad news?

                    COACH GRIFFIN
          Could be very good.

                    COACH WESTFIELD(VO)
          That's what I like to hear coach.

Coach Westfield comes down from the bird's nest and walks over to Coach Griffin. In the background we see Bucky handing the shoes to Ronnie and running off.

> COACH WESTFIELD (CONT'D)
> What is it coach?

> COACH GRIFFIN
> You know that kid down there? Ronnie Piper.

> COACH WESTFIELD
> (looking down at Ronnie)
> Never seen him before. Where is he from?

> COACH GRIFFIN
> Jefferson High School. It's in LA somewhere.

> COACH WESTFIELD
> Jefferson High School? Oh yea that's Cecil Thompson's school. This must be the kid he was telling me about. As a favor to him I said I'll let him try and walk-on. He said because their athletic program was in such shambles, no other school would even give him a look. Said the kid had more raw potential than anyone he has ever coached.

> COACH GRIFFIN
> Didn't he coach you?

> COACH WESTFIELD
> (seriously)
> Yes he did...as well as at least a dozen All-Americans.

> COACH GRIFFIN
> A dozen? Wow. What the heck was he doing coaching at Jefferson?

> COACH WESTFIELD
> Coach Thompson is one of the best high school coaches I have ever been around but more importantly he is one of the best people I have ever been around. He could have coached most anywhere he wanted in southern California, but he wanted to do what most don't. And that's to give back to the community where he grew up.
> (MORE)

                    COACH WESTFIELD (CONT'D)
               He graduated from and was a stud
               running back for Jefferson and he
               was just broken to see how far it
               had degraded. So, before he retired
               he wanted to try and resurrect the
               program. He's only been there a couple
               of years.

Ronnie finishes lacing up the shoes and walks over to the
goal line. Coach Griffin blows his whistle and Ronnie sprints
the 40 yards and then starts stretching several yards away
as the coaches talk.

                    COACH GRIFFIN
               Four point two flat coach. That's
               the fastest I've ever timed.

                    COACH WESTFIELD
               If his hands are as good as his feet,
               we just hit the jackpot.
                    (looking up at Ronnie)
               Hey Ronnie, come over here son.

Ronnie gets up and jogs over to the coaches.

                    RONNIE
               Yes coach.

                    COACH WESTFIELD
               When was the last time you were timed?

                    RONNIE
               The beginning of last football season.

                    COACH WESTFIELD
               What did you run?

                    RONNIE
               Four three, four four I really don't
               remember for sure. Nobody ever took
               it very seriously.

                    COACH WESTFIELD
               Well Mr. Piper you just ran a four
               two oh. That's All-American speed my
               friend and that's something that I
               take very seriously. Now go get in
               line and run some routes I want to
               see your hands.

                    RONNIE
               Yes sir coach.

Ronnie turns and starts to run off.

                          COACH WESTFIELD
                    Hey Ronnie. Impress me.

Ronnie turns back around grins at the coaches and then runs
over to the rest of his teammates.

INT. COACH BUDDY WESTFIELD'S OFFICE - LATE AFTERNOON

Coach Griffin bursts open the door and then grimaces as he
sees Coach Westfield sitting behind his desk on the telephone.
Coach Westfield immediately looks up.

                          COACH GRIFFIN
                        (mouths)
                    Sorry.

Coach Westfield holds up one finger to silence Coach Griffin.

                          COACH WESTFIELD
                        (phone)
                    Yes, Cecil I'll take good care of
                    him. But if he is as good as I think
                    he can be, he'll be taking care of
                    me for the next four years. I'll
                    call you next week and tell you how
                    he's doing. Good talking to you coach.
                    Goodbye.

                          COACH GRIFFIN
                    Coach Thompson?

                          COACH WESTFIELD
                        (shaking his head
                         affirmatively)
                    I called him to ask if Ronnie had
                    any baggage I needed to be concerned
                    about. He told me he was one of the
                    cleanest kids he knew. No drugs, no
                    alcohol, goes to church every Sunday,
                    the whole nine yards. And his name
                    is Pippen not Piper.

KNOCK on the door.

                          COACH WESTFIELD (CONT'D)
                    Come in.

Ronnie enters the room.

                          RONNIE
                    You wanted to see me coach?

                          COACH WESTFIELD
                    Yes, Ronnie have a seat.

Ronnie walks over to and sits in a chair across the desk from Coach Westfield.

                COACH WESTFIELD (CONT'D)
        Ronnie I just got off the phone with
        Coach Thompson. He had nothing but
        good things to say about you.

                RONNIE
            (looking somewhat
            embarrassed)
        Coach Thompson is a good man.

                COACH WESTFIELD
        Yes, he is and a good judge of
        character and talent. He said you
        had the attitude and brains to match
        your physical ability and to be quite
        honest with you Ronnie, that excites
        me. You really impressed me out there
        today, so much so Ronnie that I am
        going to give you a scholarship.

Ronnie's eyes get as big as silver dollars as he bites his lower lip to keep from screaming like a mad man in the middle of the office. Coach Griffin tries unsuccessfully to contain his own smile as he sees tears well up in Ronnie's eyes.

                RONNIE
        I...I don't know what to say. Thanks
        ...but how? I thought all scholarships
        had been given out.

                COACH WESTFIELD
        They had been, but it seems that one
        of my recruits from San Jose likes
        the night life a little too much for
        my liking. He was arrested for DUI
        the night before classes began so I
        pulled his scholarship.

                RONNIE
        That's so awesome!...I mean...uh
        ...not the DUI but that you are doing
        this for me.

                COACH WESTFIELD
        I also informed the cafeteria manager
        that you won't be needing that job
        after all. He was disappointed
        because he said he really liked you
        and asked if you could at least finish
        the week out so that he could schedule
        your replacement. Those guys over
                (MORE)

                    COACH WESTFIELD (CONT'D)
               there did me a huge favor by giving
               you a job so I need you to do just
               that.

                         RONNIE
               Yes, for sure and thanks again Coach.
               You won't regret this.

                    COACH WESTFIELD
               I'm sure I won't.

Ronnie turns around and starts walking to the door.

                    COACH WESTFIELD (CONT'D)
               And Ronnie...

Ronnie turns back around.

                    COACH WESTFIELD (CONT'D)
               Why didn't you tell me your name was
               Pippen and not Piper?

                         RONNIE
                    (smiling)
               You know the old saying, "I don't
               care what you call me as long as you
               call my play"...or something like
               that.

                    COACH WESTFIELD
                    (smiling)
               Or something like that.

INT. MOODY HALL-EARLY EVENING

Ronnie walks down the hall to his room loaded down with a
backpack and two athletic bags, one draped over each shoulder.
The hall is absent of any activity. Ronnie takes his key out
and unlocks and then opens the door.

The room is pitch black. Ronnie sets down his bags and reaches
to flip on the light. Out of the darkness a very large figure
tackles Ronnie sending him ferociously to the ground. Three
more shadows then dive on top of the pile and all begin
pounding with their fists all over Ronnie's body.

After about 45 seconds of the free-for-all Troy turns on the
light switch revealing a large poster taped on the wall with
sloppy letters stating "Ronnie you da Man!!!"

Louis, Paul, and Willie get off the back of Ronnie and help
him up to his feet.

                    LOUIS
            (high-fiving Ronnie)
          We heard the news real deal. No more
          gettin' up at 5 and slopping eggs.

                    PAUL
            (giving the forearm)
          Like Johnny Paycheck said, "Take
          this job and shove it baby".

                    RONNIE
          Thanks man. Actually, the job wasn't
          that bad. It was just a few idiots
          that made it tough. I just can't
          believe Coach 'shipped me out of the
          blue like that.

                    WILLIE
          Out of the blue? You run a four two
          forty and don't drop a single pass
          thrown at you. Coach Westfield was
          just afraid UCLA would catch wind
          and steal you away right from under
          their noses.

                    TROY
          That's right Ronnie. You were amazing
          out there. You are getting what you
          deserve.

                    RONNIE
          Thanks guys. That means a lot to me.

                    LOUIS
          Unload your stuff man. We're heading
          to Killa Wings to celebrate your
          freedom.

                    RONNIE
          Man I can't tonight. I still have
          one more morning of slopping eggs.

                    TROY
          That's too bad. I thought coach would
          get you out of it.

                    RONNIE
          I'm so jacked up about the scholarship
          I really don't mind. Besides I have
          a little unfinished business to take
          care of.

                    LOUIS
          Oh well we'll just have to celebrate
          your freedom without you. Let's get
          outta here homies.

All the guys enthusiastically start leaving the room in
anticipation of the feast of wings that awaits them. Troy is
the last one in line, and as he is just about to walk out
through the door he turns, smiles and shakes his fist and
then points at Ronnie. Ronnie mouths the word thanks and
shakes his fist back.

INT. CAFETERIA - MORNING

A clock on the wall shows 6:23. There is a line of about 50
students waiting to go into the serving area. Ted and his
posse walk to the front of the line and start talking to the
rather homely but sweet looking girl that is first in line.

                    TED
          Hi. My name is Ted Walters and the
          only reason I am talking to you right
          now is to make the people standing
          in line think that I know you, so
          they won't get mad when my friends
          and I break in front of you. Have a
          good day, and I hope I never have to
          talk to you for the rest of my life.

Ted and his two friends start laughing and cut in front of
the rather embarrassed girl. Alejandra walks up to the sliding
glass door from the inside and smiling rolls open the door.

                    TED (CONT'D)
          What's the deal Maria? It's only
          6:25.
               (in a fake Spanish
                accent)
          What about de bossman?

                    ALEJANDRA
               (smiling)
          I will take my shances.

Alejandra moves out of their way and the guys walk into the
serving area.

INT. SERVING AREA -- CONTINUOUS

Ronnie is standing behind the egg tray wearing his white
serving outfit.

                    ALEJANDRA(VO)
          Jew boys have a good breakfast.

                    SMART ALECK #2
               What is her problem?

                    SMART ALECK #1
               Probably two much tequila last night.

                    TED
               Give me the usual, lunch lady.

Ronnie dishes out a hefty spoonful of eggs from the tray and
puts them on Ted's plate.

                    SMART ALECK #2
               All the way around, lunch lady.

Smart Alecks #1 & #2 reach out their plates, and Ronnie again
dishes out two large spoonfuls of eggs from the back of the
tray and puts them on their plates. Ted then looks curiously
at Ronnie's see-through shirt pocket.

                    TED
                    (laughing)
               What is that? Exlax?

Looking surprised Ronnie immediately looks down and reactively
puts his hand over his pocket. Then quickly takes the laxative
package out of his shirt pocket and stuffs it into his front
pants pocket.

                    SMART ALECK #2
               (laughing) What a dipwad!

                    SMART ALECK #1
                    (laughing)
               Not enough bran in your diet?

                    TED
               Don't take too many of those things
               or you'll be on the dumper all day
               ...loser.

Ted and the gang start walking down the service line. Ronnie
ignores their comments and looks at the girl next up as Ted
and his boys walk down the line.

                    GIRL
               I'll take some eggs please.

                    RONNIE
               I'm sorry, I need to get another
               tray. It'll be just a sec.

                    GIRL
               (curiously pointing) What's wrong
               with those?

                    RONNIE
               (smiling)
          Trust me...you don't want any of
          these eggs.

The girl looks down the line at Ted and then back at Ronnie.

                    GIRL
               (smiling)
          I think I'll just have a bowl of
          cereal.

                    RONNIE
               (winks)
          Good choice.

INT. DINING AREA -- CONTINUOUS

Ted and his friends sit down at a table by themselves and
begin to eat.

                    SMART ALECK #1
          So Ted...are your parents gonna make
          you work on campus this year?

                    TED
          What do you mean? They never make me
          get a job.

                    SMART ALECK #2
          Yeah, but they always threaten you
          with the old "Ted if you don't get
          your act together, we're going to
          make you pay for your school" bit.

                    TED
          The key word there is threaten. They
          never follow through. It's been that
          way my whole life.
               (mockingly)
          "Ted if you don't clean your room,
          your friends can't come over. Ted if
          you hit your sister again, no video
          games for a week. Ted if I get another
          call from your teacher, we're going
          to send you to military school."
          Yeah right...I've never taken their
          threats seriously. All I had to do
          was start crying and say
               (fake crying voice)
          "I'm sorry. I'll never do it again.
          Just give me one more chance. I
          promise I'll be good from now on".
          Man, after that Academy award winning
                         (MORE)

                        TED (CONT'D)
            performance, my friends would be
            over playing Nintendo by noon.

Smart Aleck #1 starts squirming in his chair.

                        SMART ALECK #2
            What's your deal?

                        SMART ALECK #1
            Dude...I've got a major fart brewing.

                        TED
            Well let it fly somewhere else. I'm
            trying to eat here.

                        SMART ALECK #1
            Too late. Here it comes.

Smart Aleck #1 grimaces his face and then relaxes it with a sigh. Immediately a look of shock and embarrassment replaces his look of relief.

                        SMART ALECK #1 (CONT'D)
            Aw man.

                        SMART ALECK #2
                  (holding his nose)
            That is the worst fart I have ever...

Ted picks up his tray and starts to go to another table.

                        TED
                  (interrupting)
            I'm not going to eat with your
            nastiness. You better check your
            drawers.

Smart Aleck #1 gets up with his hand covering his butt and starts running for the exit.

                        SMART ALECK #1
                  (excitedly)
            I think I freaking crapped my pants!

Alejandra is strategically stationed by the exit door and opens it for Smart Aleck #1 as he goes racing by.

                        ALEJANDRA
                  (smiling)
            Jew have a good day now.

Alejandra watches Smart Aleck #1 sprint into the bathroom and then she refocuses her attention on the table Ted and Smart Aleck #2 moved to.

                    ALEJANDRA (CONT'D)
               One down. Two to go.

Ted and Smart Aleck #2 resume eating at the table by
themselves.

                    SMART ALECK #2
               That might have been the sickest
               thing I have ever witnessed.

                    TED
               We are going to be giving him crap
               about that for a loooooong time.
               No pun intended haha.

                    SMART ALECK #2
               Yea what a...

A sudden look of distress appears on the face of Smart Aleck
#2.

                    TED
               No. Not you too. You guys are such
               losers.

He immediately jolts up from the table and runs past Alejandra
out the exit door.

                    ALEJANDRA
               (smiling) Uno mas.

Ted shakes his head and starts back eating. While he has a
spoonful of eggs in his mouth he looks up and sees Ronnie
spying at him around the corner of the serving area exit
door. Ronnie sees Ted looking his way and immediately ducks
out of his viewing.

                    TED
               What the heck is he looking at?

Ted spoons up another bite of eggs and puts it in his mouth.
While he is chewing a loud rumbling sound comes from his
belly. He looks down at his stomach and then immediately
looks up towards the serving area exit door where Ronnie had
been spying on him.

CLOSE UP ON TED'S FACE

                    TED (CONT'D)
               You black piece of...

Ted grimaces and then puts his left arm around his stomach.
He stands up and throws his plate of eggs on the floor.

                    TED (CONT'D)
               (Yelling)
          Agghhhh!!

CUT TO INT OF SERVING AREA

Ronnie is standing with his back against the wall by the
exit door out of sight from the people in dining area.

                    RONNIE
               (In a high voice)
          Busted!

CUT TO INT OF DINING ROOM

Ted is walking briskly with his left arm around his stomach
heading for the exit.

                    TED
               (yelling)
          I'm gonna get you, you black piece
          of garbage.

A huge black arm grabs Ted from behind and spins him around.
Ted whips around like a rag doll and stares up at a giant
well-built African American male.

                    BLACK MALE
          Who you gonna get white boy?

                    TED
          Sure the heck not you!

                    BLACK MALE
          Well then who white boy?

                    TED
          Listen man...I'd love to stand here
          and discuss it with you but trust me
          I got to go.

                    BLACK MALE
          White boy you're not going anywhere
          'till I'm finished with you.

Ted grimaces again and lets out a nasty sounding explosion.

                    BLACK MALE (CONT'D)
               (wincing)
          Yo white boy I'm finished with you.

Ted lets out a groan and starts running to the exit door.

                    ALEJANDRA
               (sarcastically)
          Que pasa senor. Do the eggs disagree
          with you?

Ted clinches his teeth at Alejandra then lets out another
groan then runs into the bathroom.

INT. BILLINGHAM CLASSROOM - MORNING

Class has begun and Professor Billingham is up front
lecturing. Ted and the boys come walking into class looking
very squeamish.

                    PROFESSOR BILLINGHAM
          Young men! Have you already forgot
          my rules about coming in late? Out
          in the hall you go. Sit in the chairs
          outside the door and you may listen
          from there.

Ted and the boys turn around and embarrassingly walk out
into the hall and pull up the waiting chairs up close to the
door.

                    PROFESSOR BILLINGHAM (CONT'D)
          Now where we?

Billingham shuffles through his notes.

                    PROFESSOR BILLINGHAM (CONT'D)
          Ah yes, we were listing out the great
          American explorers of the 20th
          century. Number three is the great
          Admiral Robert Peary. The Admiral
          took a group of Inuit Eskimos and
          conquered the North Pole on April 6,
          1909. Admiral Peary was the first
          human being to ever step foot on the
          North Pole although several have
          accomplished this feat since that
          time...But he was the first. Number
          four on the list...

                    RONNIE
               (murmuring)
          Allegedly.

Immediately Billingham looks over the top of his glasses and
peers at Ronnie.

                    PROFESSOR BILLINGHAM
          Allegedly? Allegedly?
               (MORE)

> PROFESSOR BILLINGHAM (CONT'D)
> Would you like to elaborate on your disruption, or would you like to just sit there and keep looking foolish?

> RONNIE
> Well sir isn't it debatable whether he actually made it all the way to the North Pole?

> PROFESSOR BILLINGHAM
> Yes, there is a debate. Among the uneducated and uninformed.

There is a snickering around the classroom.

> RONNIE
> And even if he did make it all the way, there was a member of his party that you failed to recognize that claims he went ahead scouting for Admiral Peary and **he** actually was the first to set foot on the North Pole...I believe his name was Henson...uh yes Matthew Henson.

> PROFESSOR BILLINGHAM
> Oh, I see. I know where this is going. Sticking up for the black man.

More snickering.

> RONNIE
> No, I'm just sticking up for what some believe is the truth.

Some ooowing from the class.

> PROFESSOR BILLINGHAM
> Like I said before this is only a debate among the uneducated and uninformed.

> MALE STUDENT #1
> Would you consider Dr. E Miles Standish of the California Institute of Technology to be a part of the uneducated and uninformed? He rejected Peary's claim altogether.

> PROFESSOR BILLINGHAM
> Where did you hear such poppycock?

                    MALE STUDENT #1
               I just googled it.

More snickering.

                    PROFESSOR BILLINGHAM
               Googled it? Googled it? You would
               believe what you read on the internet
               or heard from a football player from
               a low-rent-ghetto black high school
               over a tenured professor with over
               25 years experience? Please sir you
               are very naive, and might I say
               intellectually challenged!

Male student #1 looks defeated and Billingham glares back over at Ronnie.

                    PROFESSOR BILLINGHAM (CONT'D)
               So, you like to stick up for the
               truth do you? I know a little bit
               about your crime ridden high school-
               consistently placing dead last year
               after year in average SAT scores. It
               seems there is not a lot of truth
               being taught there. As a matter of
               fact, let us all join in Mr. Pippen's
               pursuit of the truth. Tomorrow we
               will be learning about American
               inventors of the 20th century so to
               get a jump start on his noble
               endeavor, everyone will need to have
               turned in by the start of class in
               the morning a 3 page single spaced
               report on a great American inventor.
               And in honor of Mr. Pippen, everyone
               must write on the very dignified
               peanut farmer George Washington
               Carver.
                    (dismissal bell rings)
               And I am sure Mr. Pippen this will
               be no problem for you with all the
               exceptional historical teaching I am
               sure you were taught at Jefferson
               High.

The class starts to rumble with animosity toward Ronnie as they are leaving class because of the extra assignment.

                    PROFESSOR BILLINGHAM (CONT'D)
               And remember Ronnie, I'm not talking
               about the country's first president.

The class erupts in laughter.

PROFESSOR BILLINGHAM (CONT'D)
Just making sure you do not get
confused.

Ronnie stops and turns around.

RONNIE
(sarcastically)
So, you're not talking about the
first president? Then who could you
be...oh wait George Washington
Carver. Isn't he the guy who was
born into slavery in January of 1864
in Missouri, I believe?
And after graduating from Minneapolis
High School wasn't he accepted into
Highland College in Kansas but was
denied admission when they found out
he was black?
Can you imagine that? Racism? Wasn't
he the first African American to
graduate from and later teach at
Iowa State University? And wasn't
he invited by Booker T Washington
himself to head up the Tuskegee
Institute's Agricultural Department
where he taught there for almost 50
years developing a crop rotation
that revolutionized southern
agriculture?

A number of students sit back down in their seats, pull out
their notebooks and start frantically writing down notes.

RONNIE (CONT'D)
And didn't he discover over 300 uses
for peanuts and hundreds more for
sweet potatoes, pecans and soybeans?
Wasn't he inducted into the Hall of
Fame for Great Americans in 1977 and
into the National Inventors Hall of
Fame in 1990? And as a deeply
religious man, did he not compile a
list of 8 virtues that he wanted his
students to live by? "Be clean both
inside and out. Neither look up to
the rich nor down on the poor. Lose,
if need be, without whining. Win
without bragging. Always be
considerate of women, children, and
older people. Be too brave to lie.
Be too generous to cheat. Take your
share of the world and let others
take theirs". Wasn't the epitaph
(MORE)

                              RONNIE (CONT'D)
                    over his grave "He could have added
                    fortune to fame, but caring for
                    neither, he found happiness and honor
                    in being helpful to the world."

Professor Billingham slams shut his notebook. Ronnie looks
dead straight into Billingham's eyes.

                              RONNIE (CONT'D)
                         (seriously)
                    And hasn't George Washington
                    Carver...the peanut farmer... been
                    my hero...ever since my grandmother
                    read me stories upon stories about
                    all the brilliant and awe-inspiring
                    world changers...no matter their
                    color...ever since I was little boy?

Ronnie breaks the stare down, picks up his books and leaves
the classroom as the students chatter about the incident.
Immediately Ted and his posse briskly walk back into the
classroom and start passionately talking to the visibly
angered Billingham. The professor devilishly grins and
slightly shakes his head in the affirmative.

EXT. PRACTICE FIELD-AFTERNOON SERIES OF SHOTS - DIFFERENT
DAYS

A montage of shots is shown of the team outfitted in practice
gear going through drills.

Man in the middle

Monkey rolls

The gauntlet

Cone drills

Team bear crawl

INT. LOCKER ROOM - LATE AFTERNOON

The team is finishing up showering and changing into street
clothes. Troy, Ronnie, Louis, Paul and Willie are all changing
in the same general area.

                              LOUIS
                    So fellas what's the big plans for
                    tonight?

                              WILLIE
                    Seriously Louis you have to ask?
                         (MORE)

                    WILLIE (CONT'D)
          It's Tuesday night you know what
          that means!

Willie looks over at Paul and they say in unison.

                    WILLIE/PAUL
               (enthusiastically)
          Half price lanes and 2 for 1
          cheeseburgers at Buckaroo Bowling.

Willie and Paul high five. Louis shake his head in the affirmative.

                    LOUIS
          Hey I'm down. What about you Troy?

                    TROY
          I've got nothing else to do. Ronnie?

                    RONNIE
          Sorry guys but I have a big test in
          the morning in a class where the
          prof hates me and I need to finish
          up studying.

                    TROY
          Hates you? Why?

                    RONNIE
          No reason really.

                    PAUL
          Oh cmon! I heard you made the dude
          look like a lost little schoolgirl
          when he tried to embarrass you.

                    RONNIE
          I didn't intend to but I've been
          around bullies all my life and usually
          they're just cowards when they get
          pushed back.

                    TROY
          Well you don't need to be pushing
          your professors. I need you around
          all four years man. You push the
          wrong one and you'll be back in LA.

                    RONNIE
          I guess you're right...What time you
          guys planning to be back anyway?

Willie looks over at Paul.

                    WILLIE
               (sarcastically)
          Oh I'm sure we'll be back by
          9:00...right Paul?

                    PAUL
               (sarcastically)
          For sure! That will give you plenty
          of time to study for the big old
          test! Heck I'll even drive. You'll
          have your own private chauffeur for
          the evening.

EXT. HIGHWAY -- EVENING

A very large and jacked up pickup truck with all the windows
down is cruising down the highway. The beginning "dun dun ta
dun ta dun dun" of Shania Twain's "Feel Like a Woman" is
blasting in the background.

INT. PAUL'S TRUCK -- EVENING

Paul and Willie are in the front seats and Troy, Ronnie, and
Louis are cramped in the back. "Feel Like a Woman" is still
playing with Paul singing every word on mark. Willie is
shaking his head in rhythm and Ronnie, Troy and Louis are
staring at Paul in disbelief.

                    PAUL
               (singing off key)
          Oh, oh, oh, get in the action. Feel
          the attraction. Color my hair, do
          what I dare Oh, oh, oh, I wanna be
          free-yeah.To feel the way I feel
          Man, I feel like a woman

                    RONNIE
               (exasperated)
          Seriously?

                    PAUL
          It's only a song!

Paul pulls into the parking lot under a large neon sign
flashing "Twofer Tuesday at the World Famous Buckaroo Bowl.

INT. BUCKAROO BOWLING -- EVENING

The bowling alley is very crowded with loud music blasting
in the background. The boys are bowling on two side by side
lanes.

SERIES OF SHOTS

Bowling between the legs.

Bowling between the legs.

Bowling an 8-pound speed ball.

Bowling behind the back.

Bowling two balls at a time.

Bowling opposite hand.

Bowling blind folded.

Louis is shown wolfing down a greasy cheeseburger with the grease dripping off the burger after each bite. Troy keeps glancing to his right staring at an attractive girl NICOLE HOLLOMAN bowling with a cute freckle faced 7-year-old boy SAMUEL.

                    RONNIE
Troy...Hey Troy!

Troy snaps his head around after being broken from his daze.

                    TROY
Uh...yea.

                    RONNIE
What do you keep staring at?

Troy flips his head to the right.

                    TROY
That girl over there.

                    RONNIE
Which girl over there?

                    TROY
Lane 22.

                    RONNIE
Yea she's smoking hot.

                    TROY
No...its not just that. There's something different...I mean...I don't know.

                    RONNIE
          Well I haven't met Michelle yet, but
          I'm pretty sure she wouldn't be too
          happy with you ogling over some random
          chic in a bowling alley. You've been
          staring at her all night.

                    TROY
          I'm not ogling. I really don't even
          know what that means. It's just that
          this girl she...she...I don't know.

                    RONNIE
          Well I, do know it's the last frame
          and it's your turn, and I've got to
          get at least some studying in tonight.

Troy stands up, walks over to the ball return, finds his
ball, and stands on the approach. He then turns around and
looks at Paul.

                    TROY
          If I strike, I'm the DJ for the ride
          back. If I don't you are.

                    PAUL
              (grinning)
          Anything you say.

Ronnie, Louis, and Willie immediately start a series of
encouragements and begin whooping it up in support of Troy's
bet. Troy turns back around and rolls the ball which hits
perfectly in the pocket. All the pins explode and flash about
except for the lone 10 pin which is left standing strong.
Troy drops his head, and the boys let out a simultaneous
moan.

                    PAUL (CONT'D)
              (matter-of-factly)
          I hope you boys like Loretta Lynn.

The boys start to gather their things together to leave.
Troy looks up and sees that Nicole has already left. He then
sees a sweater lying on a table in the area where she had
been bowling earlier. He walks over and grabs the sweater
and then walks to CASHIER JOE, a man in his early sixties
with a disheveled look about him.

                    TROY
          I believe the girl on lane 22 left
          this. Has she already gone?

                    CASHIER JOE
          Lane 22?
              (MORE)

                    CASHIER JOE (CONT'D)
               hmmmm...oh yea the pretty girl with
               the kid. She just left...prolly can
               catch her in the parking lot.

                    TROY
               Thanks.

EXT. PARKING LOT -- EVENING

Troy immediately sprints out to the parking lot with sweater
in hand. He runs to the right and jogs to the far end of the
parking lot. He looks left and sees Nicole and Samuel walking
to her car. They are slowly walking about 30 yards in front
of Troy. He slows down and starts walking towards them.

                    TROY
               Excuse me...Excuse me.

Nicole and Samuel keep walking.

                    TROY (CONT'D)
                    (Louder)
               Excuse me!

Nicole lifts up her hand and clicks the lock on her key as
the lights of her car flash about 10 feet in front of her.
Troy stops walking.

                    TROY (CONT'D)
                    (very loudly)
               Hey!! You left your sweater!

Nicole and Samuel get in the car and drive off as Troy stands
there with a bewildered look on his face. Troy looks left
and sees Paul's truck rapidly flying towards him.

                    WILLIE
                    (Excitedly)
               Quick jump in!

                    TROY
               What's going on?

                    PAUL
               I just got a call from Big Fridge.
               He heard Coach is doing a surprise
               bed check tonight to make sure no
               one is out passed curfew. We have 20
               minutes to be in our rooms!

                    TROY
               I've got to drop this off inside in
               case that girl comes looking for it.

Ronnie springs his head up from the back seat.

                    RONNIE
          Troy we don't have time! Get in!
          Bring it back later!

Troy hesitates than jumps in the truck. Paul hurriedly screeches off.

INT. BILLINGHAM CLASSROOM - MORNING

The classroom is completely filled. The students are feverishly working to complete the test before class ends. Professor Billingham is standing in the front and looks down at his watch.

                    PROFESSOR BILLINGHAM
          Ten minutes.

The class begins to rustle about with panicked looks on quite a few faces. Four students get up and turn in their tests on Billingham's desk and exit the room. Billingham looks at Ted who is sitting two seats behind Ronnie, and Ted displays a soft devilish grin and ever so slightly nods his head in the affirmative. Ronnie stands up, picks up his test, and begins to walk over to Billingham's desk. After a short pause, Ted stands up, and as he is passing the seat that Ronnie just left, very covertly drops a half wadded-up sheet of paper and nudges it under Ronnie's desk. Ronnie turns in his test and then exits the class. Ted lays his test on Billingham's desk and slowly walks towards the door. Billingham looks over at Ronnie's desk with a quizzical look on his face that gets the attention of several students in the class. He walks over to his desk and bends down and picks up the paper. At this point quite a few students are watching him. He unwads the paper and as he is reading it his face immediately changes into a look of feigned rage.

                    PROFESSOR BILLINGHAM (CONT'D)
               (restrained)
          Who was sitting in this chair?

The students blankly stair at Billingham not wanting to rat out Ronnie.

                    PROFESSOR BILLINGHAM (CONT'D)
               (loudly)
          I said who was sitting in this chair?!

                    STUDENT (O.S.)
          The football player.

                    SMART ALECK #1
                (excitedly)
            Yea! Ronnie Pippen! Ronnie Pippen
            was sitting there!

                    PROFESSOR BILLINGHAM
                (looking down at note)
            Well Mr. Pippen has just graced this
            classroom with his presence for the
            last time.

EXT. PRACTICE FIELD-AFTERNOON SERIES OF SHOTS - SAME DAY

A montage of shots is shown of the team outfitted in practice gear.

A full offense and defense are on the field, the ball is snapped, and Willie sprints towards the B gap, breaks down, and blows up the running back.

A full offense and defense are on the field, the ball is snapped, and a close up of Louis and Paul getting after it is shown.

A full offense and defense are on the field the ball is snapped to Troy and he hits a flying Ronnie who is running a skinny post 40 yards down the field.

Half the team is on one sideline and half on the other sideline. A whistle is blown and one side sprints across the field. A soon as the last one makes it across another whistle is blown and the other half sprints across the field. The whole time the coaches are screaming "encouragements" mainly to get the "fat boys" across the field.

                    COACH WESTFIELD
            Coach Griffin please get the boys
            huddled up on the 50.

                    COACH GRIFFIN
                (loudly)
            All right Bearcats take a knee on
            the 50. Come on let's go! On the
            hop!

The players sprint to mid-field, take off their helmets, and take a knee.

                    COACH WESTFIELD
            Tomorrow is a big day. Yes sir, a
            really big day. For some it will be
            the last time they will ever play in
            a season opening game. For others,
            it will be the first time they will
                            (MORE)

                    COACH WESTFIELD (CONT'D)
               have collided heads in a Division I
               college football game. You won't
               sleep much tonight. No...and there'll
               be a big pit in your stomach as your
               nerves wrestle with your courage as
               you eat your breakfast. Your emotions
               will be soaring through the roof
               when you run out onto the field as
               80,000 rabid Bearcat fans are
               screaming for you.
                    (pause)
               But when that whistle blows gentleman,
               it's time to put all that aside and
               go to work. We all have one mission.
               Do you know what that is?
                    (silence)
               I said do you know what that is!

The majority of the team yells out "to win the game!"

                    COACH WESTFIELD (CONT'D)
               Yes, that's right. Our sole mission
               is to win the game. And we will do
               that with strength, intelligence,
               speed and integrity. We will be a
               complete team.
                    (pause)
               And, that team will be led by a
               freshman quarterback.

Coach Westfield tosses a football over to Troy.

                    COACH WESTFIELD (CONT'D)
               Can you lead this team to a national
               championship son?

                    TROY
                    (Confidently)
               Yes sir, I can.

                    COACH WESTFIELD
               Then do it!

Coach Griffin stands up and pumps his fist.

                    COACH GRIFFIN
               Let's all do it!

The team in unison steps up, starts jumping and shouting,
and acting wild in uncontrolled pandemonium.

                    COACH WESTFIELD
               Ok, hit the showers and go to bed
               early! Big day tomorrow!
                    (Under his breath)
               Big day.

INT. DORM ROOM - NIGHT

The lights are off in Troy and Ronnie's dorm room except for
the lamp over Ronnie's desk. Ronnie is sitting at his desk
getting some last-minute homework done, and Troy is lying on
his bunk staring at the ceiling and wearing headphones
listening to music. Troy sits up in his bunk and takes his
headphones off.

                    TROY
               Coach was right. I'm not going to be
               able to sleep. I'll probably be
               tossing and turning all night.

Ronnie turns around in his chair.

                    RONNIE
               Not me man. In five minutes I'll be
               done studying. Then I'm gonna go
               wash my face, brush my teeth, get in
               bed, say a little prayer and then
               I'll be out like a light.

                    TROY
               How can you do that? I mean your
               first college game...how can you do
               that?

Ronnie gets up and moves his chair closer to Troy's bunk.

                    TROY (CONT'D)
               What if I go out there and stink the
               place up? What if the speed of the
               game at this level is just too fast
               for me? What if I just freeze? I can
               see the headlines in the paper. Troy
               "The Gun"? No Troy "The Dud"! What
               if...

                    RONNIE
                 (abruptly)
               Stop!

Troy that's just not going to happen. You ARE that good.
You'll be able to handle anything thrown at you and down
deep you know it.

TROY
Man I hope you're right...So you're not anxious or nervous even a little bit?

RONNIE
(smiling)
Yea..a little bit. But that's where I have a major advantage on you and most people I'll be playing against.

TROY
How's that?

RONNIE
When I was young, my mama told me the one advantage of being poor is that when you've got nothing to lose you've got nothing to lose. That has always pushed me into trying new things and never being afraid of failure. I'm gonna play tomorrow fearless...like I've got nothing to lose.

TROY
That explains how you can go across the middle of the field so effortlessly when most receivers have alligator arms worried about the safety bearing down on them.

RONNIE
Now you know my secret.

TROY
That I do...So I go out there tomorrow and play like I've got nothing to lose.

Ronnie stands up and gives Troy a love tap on his chest.

RONNIE
You've got it. Now go to sleep. I've got to finish up my chemistry.

Troy lays back down. Ronnie takes his chair back over to his desk, sits down, and starts studying again.

RONNIE (CONT'D)
Troy "The Dud" Dunn. Hey I kinda like it.

Troy smiles than closes his eyes.

EXT. NCU STADIUM - AFTERNOON

Oregon Ducks vs Northern Californian University Bobcats A panning of the stands shows Troy's family nervously waiting for the kickoff as the players are warming up. Michelle is noticeably missing. The Oregon Duck's kicker kicks the ball into the NCU end zone, and a Bearcat player catches it and takes a knee. The Bearcat offense takes the field. Troy is at the sidelines getting final instructions from Coach Westfield who is wearing a headset. Troy trots over to the huddle of his waiting teammates.

>   CLIFF
>   (Softly)
>   Here we go.

SERIES OF SHOTS - SAME GAME

Troy is in under center. Louis snaps him the ball then explodes off the line pancaking the left defensive tackle. Troy hands off to the halfback on the left side for a halfback dive. The halfback runs through the gaping hole courtesy of Louis, sheds a defender, and then gets tackled resulting in a 18 yard gain.

Troy is in shotgun. He receives the snap. A heavy rush is coming from the right side. He rolls out left then throws the ball to the sideline. Ronnie makes a great diving catch, keeping both feet in bounds for a 15 yard gain.

Troy is under center. He receives the snap. He fakes the handoff to the running back who gets rocked by the linebacker at the line who bit on the fake. Ronnie runs 10 yards then cuts outside on a corner route then a second cut inside for a skinny post route. The safety bites on the first cut. Troy scrambles to his right. He throws a bomb down the middle of the field. Ronnie runs under the pass and sprints untouched to the end zone.

INT. GRANDMA'S HOUSE - EARLY EVENING

Grandma and Big Daddy are on the edge of their seats as they watch the game on Grandma's small b&w tv. As usual Grandma is in her rocker, and Big Daddy is on the couch.

>   TV ANNOUNCER KEITH GALLAGHER (O.S.)
>   Dunn scrambles. Pippen is streaking
>   to the end zone. Touchdown!

Grandma and Big Daddy immediately spring out of their chairs and hug each other all the while screaming. Big Daddy releases his death grip on Grandma and starts doing a "thriller" with a mix in of a moon walk Michael Jackson impersonation around the room.

SERIES OF SHOTS - SAME GAME

The Duck quarterback is under center. He receives the snap and tosses the ball to the right for a halfback sweep. Willie sheds a block and comes off the edge to make an explosive hit on the halfback for a loss of five yards.

The Duck quarterback is in shotgun. He receives the snap and fakes a hand off to his halfback. He rolls right and looks at a well-covered wide receiver. He pulls up to pass and gets rocked by Paul who is torpedoing in on his blind side.

Troy is under center 15 yards away from pay dirt. He receives the snap, fakes a hand off to his fullback and throws a fade to a leaping Pippen. Ronnie comes down with a foot in bounds and the referee signals touchdown.

> TV ANNOUNCER KEITH GALLAGHER (CONT'D)
> This freshman duo of Dunn and Pippen looks to be the lethal combination that Coach Buddy Westfield has been looking for, for years.

> TV ANNOUNCER BART HACKETT (O.S.)
> Oh yes it does. Folks hold on to your hats because the next four years of NCU football are going to be quite exciting!

EXT. OUTSIDE THE STADIUM - EVENING

Friends and family wait for the players to come out. Rebecca & Cliff are there to greet Troy. Troy and Ronnie walk out together chatting. As they approach, Rebecca briskly walks over to Troy and gives him a big hug. Cliff stands there grinning ear to ear.

> REBECCA
> I'm so proud of you snukums.

Troy glances over at Ronnie and sees him grinning. Cliff breaks in the embrace and gives Troy a quick hug himself.

> CLIFF
> Proud of you son.

Troy looks over at Ronnie who is standing awkwardly beside the lovefest.

> TROY
> Oh yeah. Mom, Dad, this is Ronnie Pippen. Ronnie, this is Mom and Dad.

Cliff reaches out and shakes Ronnie's hand.

                    RONNIE
          Glad to meet you Sir.

                    CLIFF
          Great game out there today. You made
          my boy look good.

                    RONNIE
          Well, you know that's my job.

Rebecca extends her hand, and Ronnie gingerly shakes it.

                    RONNIE (CONT'D)
          And glad to meet you as well maam.

                    REBECCA
          Very nice to...

Rebecca looks at Ronnie's arm and sees a gash jagging across his forearm.

                    REBECCA (CONT'D)
          Oh my. What happened? Are you Ok?

                    RONNIE
              (grinning)
          It's nothing. Just got cut by a
          corner's helmet.

                    REBECCA
          Well, did you let the trainer look
          at it?

                    TROY
          Mom, its ok! He'll be fine.

                    REBECCA
          I just don't want it to get infected.

                    RONNIE
          I'll be fine maam. But I do appreciate
          the concern.

                    TROY
          Soooo. Where is Michelle?

                    REBECCA
          She told me to tell you that she
          really wanted to come, but she has a
          big test on Monday and really needed
          to study.

Cliff rolls his eyes.

                    TROY
          Wow I guess she's finally going to
          take her studies seriously.

                    CLIFF
          Sure thing sport. Hey Ronnie, do you
          have plans for the evening? We have
          an extra room, and Rebecca and I
          would love for you to stay over.

                    RONNIE
          I would like to but...

                    TROY
               (interrupting)
          Oh stop. He has no plans and would
          love to spend the night at our humble
          abode.

                    RONNIE
          I just don't want to intrude.

Rebecca walks over and hooks her arm around Ronnie's as they
all walk to the parking lot.

                    REBECCA
          No intrusion at all Ronnie. We would
          love to have you. We can get to
          know you better, and you can tell us all
          about college life living with my
          son.

                    TROY
          Ronnie...don't forget about our code
          of silence.

                    RONNIE
          Oh I won't. For the right price I
          can forget about a lot of things.

Ronnie looks over at Cliff.

                    RONNIE (CONT'D)
          But for the right price, I can
          remember a lot of things as well.

                    CLIFF
          I like this guy.

                    TROY
          What a sellout.

The four walk a little further in the parking lot.

                    TROY (CONT'D)
          Ok, we'll just meet ya'll at the
          house. I'm parked way over behind
          the gym, and I've got to go over and
          say something to my linemen.

                    CLIFF
          Yeah, they saved your bacon quite a
          few times.

                    TROY
          Yeah they did. See ya'll at the house.

The four part ways and start heading in opposite directions.

                    RONNIE
          Saved your bacon? Snukums?

Troy chuckles.

                    RONNIE (CONT'D)
          White folks are just weird!

INT. TROY'S CAR - EVENING

Troy and Ronnie are riding the car listening to the radio. Troy spots Michelle's car in the parking lot of a local hot spot called Full Throttle as they drive by.

                    TROY
          What the...?

That's Michelle's car.

Troy makes a U-turn and pulls his car into the overflowing parking lot.

EXT. PARKING LOT OF FULL THROTTLE - EVENING

Troy and Ronnie briskly walk to the front door.

INT. FULL THROTTLE - EVENING

Troy sees a drunken Michelle dirty dancing with a handsome preppie guy. Troy immediately walks over to her, grabs her by the arm, and twirls her around.

                    TROY
          Michelle! What are you doing?

                    MICHELLE
              (slurred)
          You know exactly what I'm doing!

The preppie jumps in front of Michelle in a threatening manner.

>> PREPPIE
>> You better start being nice to my date.

Looks back at Michelle.

>> PREPPIE (CONT'D)
>> What's your name again sweet cakes?

Troy steps up towards preppie.

>> TROY
>> Her name is Michelle and she sure the heck is not your date Dapper Dan!

>> PREPPIE
>> Well she is for the night. Isn't that right sweet cakes?

Michelle staggers forward.

>> MICHELLE
>> You know you're never around anymore Troy. You're always so busy with football, church, school and everything else except me. I need more attention, and you just won't give it to me. I just need more.

>> TROY
>> Yeah. That's the problem. You always need more.

Troy turns around and starts to walk back towards the door with Ronnie following.

>> MICHELLE
>> We're finished Troy! Finished!

Troy just keeps walking with no acknowledgement.

>> MICHELLE (CONT'D)
>> I cheated on you three times!

The bar patrons start whooping and hollering. Troy stops and slowly turns around.

>> TROY
>> I never cheated on you.

Michelle bursts into tears. Troy and Ronnie walk outside the door.

EXT. PARKING LOT OF FULL THROTTLE - EVENING

Troy and Ronnie walk across the parking lot towards his car. They are followed by Preppie and three of his friends, two are white and one is black.

                    PREPPIE
          Yo superstar. Ya'll might be finished
          but me and you aren't. I don't like
          to be called Dapper Dan! You got
          that straight superstar?

Troy and Ronnie stop and the four front up to the two.

                    TROY
          Dude I really don't want...

                    PREPPIE
              (interrupting and
               condescending)
          Here we go.

                    TROY
              (slowly)
          ...to fight.
              (quickly)
          Never mind, yes I do.

Preppie steps towards Troy and the others step closer as well. Preppie's black friend looks at Ronnie.

                    BLACK FRIEND
          Yo brother, you need to back out.
          This is not your fight.

                    RONNIE
          No brother. This **is** my fight. More
          than you know.

                    PREPPIE
              (smiling)
          So superstar, since it's four of us
          and only two of you, you can take
          the first punch.

                    TROY
          Okay.

Troy immediately hits preppie in the face knocking him out cold. The remaining combatants start brawling with each other. There is a montage of fight scenes where each participant is giving and taking in equal proportion.

                    WHITE FRIEND #1
               Screw this, I'm out of here.

White friend #1 starts jogging away. The other two friends
see this and look at each other.

                    BLACK FRIEND
               Let's get out of here.

                    WHITE FRIEND #2
               Yeah.

White friend #2 looks over at preppie out cold in the parking
lot.

                    WHITE FRIEND #2 (CONT'D)
               What are we going to do with him?

                    BLACK FRIEND
               Leave him. I never liked Dapper Dan
               anyway.

White friend #2 and black friend jog off thru the parking
lot.

A bruised and slightly bloodied Troy and Ronnie stand in the
parking lot still in fight-ready position. As they watch the
friends jog away, Troy looks at Ronnie.

                    TROY
               You ready to go home?

                    RONNIE
               Yeah. I'm getting kind of hungry.

The two smile, embrace, jog over to Troy's car, and speed
away.

EXT. DUNN HOUSE - EVENING

Troy and Ronnie drive up and park in the circle drive.

INT. DUNN HOUSE - EVENING

Cliff is sitting at the dining room table with a half-eaten
sandwich in front of him. He is reading the sports section
of the local paper. Troy and Ronnie walk in the front door.
Cliff looks over the top of his reading glasses.

                    CLIFF
               You boys get lost?

                    REBECCA (O.S.)
               I hope ya'll didn't stop and get
               something to eat.

Rebecca walks into the dining room from the kitchen with a plate of sandwiches on it. She looks at the boys, gasps, puts the plate on the counter, and runs over to them. Cliff stands up.

> REBECCA (CONT'D)
> (frantically)
> Oh my what happened? Did ya'll get into a wreck? Are you hurt? Is everyone ok?

> TROY
> It's ok mom. I'm fine. Got in a little skirmish at Full Throttle but I'm fine.

> CLIFF
> Full Throttle? Why...

> REBECCA
> (interrupting)
> Why did ya'll stop there? I hate that place.

> CLIFF
> Son, what's going on?

> TROY
> Well we were coming straight home, but I saw Michelle's car in the parking lot.

Cliff drops his head and throws down the paper on the table.

> CLIFF
> (mutters under his breath)
> I knew it.

> TROY
> We go in and she's grinding on some preppie looking guy on the dance floor.

Cliff and Rebecca both cringe.

> TROY (CONT'D)
> One thing led to another and we wound up in a brawl in the parking lot with four other guys.

> CLIFF
> (excitedly)
> Four?! Ha ha...how'd they turn out?

                              REBECCA
                    Cliff! Could you not have just walked
                    away? Did you have to fight it out?

                              TROY
                    It would have been tough, mom.

Dad gathers his composure as Ronnie stands silently by.

                              CLIFF
                    Son even in tough situations like
                    that you have to learn just to walk
                    away. Sometimes your pride is your
                    worst enemy.

Troy drops his head.

                              TROY
                         (contritely)
                    I know dad. I should have just walked
                    away.

Rebecca walks over and embraces Troy.

                              REBECCA
                    Well, I'm just glad both of you are
                    ok.

Ronnie smiles but is still silent.

                              REBECCA (CONT'D)
                    I've got to get up early, so I am
                    going on to bed. Ronnie, Cliff will
                    show you where you will be sleeping.

                              RONNIE
                    Thank you.

                              REBECCA
                    I'm sure you guys will sleep through
                    breakfast, so I will cook you a good
                    lunch when ya'll wake up.

                              TROY
                    Thanks mom. You're the greatest.

                              RONNIE
                    Yes. And thanks for the sandwiches.

Rebecca smiles, turns around and walks around the corner
into the hallway. Cliff waits a few seconds then tiptoes
towards the hallway. He peers around the corner for a few
seconds. The sound of a door shutting is heard. Cliff, with
a big smile on his face, softly but quickly scampers back
over to the two boys.

                        CLIFF
                (excitedly but hushed)
            Details! Details!

                        RONNIE
                (excitedly)
            Oh, it was crazy! The white dude
            says
                (mockingly)
            its two against four, so you get the
            first punch and BAM! Troy knocks him
            out cold. Then, it was just a free
            for all.

                        TROY
            Fists were flying and and then all
            of a sudden, they just took off.

                        CLIFF
            Didn't want any more of it. Two
            against four. That's pretty
            impressive.

                        TROY
            Dad, she said she cheated on me three
            times.

                        CLIFF
            I don't doubt it. I NEVER liked that
            girl. Waaaay too uppity for me.

                        TROY
            Well it's over Dad.

                        CLIFF
            I'm sure it's for the best son but,
            I know it's gotta be painful.

                        TROY
            The funny thing is it's really not.
            I feel released.

                        RONNIE
            Well good so now you can focus on
            school and gettin me that rock.

Troy and Ronnie fist bump.

                        TROY
            That's right.

                        CLIFF
            Well Troy, tell you're WWF partner
            good night. I'm going to show him to
            his room.

Troy and Ronnie shake hugs and hold the embrace.

                    TROY
          (whispers) Thanks man.

                    RONNIE
              (whispers)
          No problem my brother.

They relax the embrace, and Troy grabs a sandwich and his bags and heads down the hallway.

                    CLIFF
          Grab your stuff and a sandwich and
          follow me.

Ronnie and Cliff walk down the hallway in the opposite direction of Troy. Cliff opens the bedroom door and the two walk in.

INT. BEDROOM #1 - EVENING

Ronnie looks around and drops his bags.

                    RONNIE
          This is really nice, sir. I really
          do appreciate the invitation.

                    CLIFF
          Just make yourself at home. Good
          night.

Cliff walks out of the room grabbing the doorknob as he passes. He starts to close the door and right before it shuts, he pops his head back in.

                    CLIFF (CONT'D)
          Ronnie.

Ronnie turns around.

                    CLIFF (CONT'D)
          I've been in those kind of situations
          before. I know all the dynamics
          involved. You could have run and
          left my boy alone. But you didn't.
          And, Rebecca and I are grateful.

                    RONNIE
          I would never have run.

                    CLIFF
          I know. Good night.

Cliff shuts the door.

INT. BEDROOM #1 - MORNING

Close up of Ronnie's face as he wakes. As his vision goes from blurry to focused, he sees he is eye to eye with an enormous Mastiff. He pushes himself backwards out of the bed and flops on the floor.

                    RONNIE
          Troy!

Troy sticks his head in the door.

                    TROY
          Max!

The dog immediately jumps off of the bed and runs out the door.

                    TROY (CONT'D)
          Mom's starting to cook. Do you want
          chicken and dumplings with turnip
          greens and pintos or a rib eye and a
          baked potato?

                    RONNIE
          Troy. Not funny.

                    TROY
          What?

                    RONNIE
          Racial jokes first thing in the
          morning.

                    TROY
          I'm being serious, dude.

                    RONNIE
              (sarcastically)
          Sure thing. Well, then I'll pick the
          steak.

                    TROY
          You don't know what you'll be missing.

                    RONNIE
          I'm sure I'll survive.

Troy leaves the room.

                    RONNIE (CONT'D)
              (muttering)
          I don't even like chicken and
          dumplings and turnip greens.

INT. DUNN HOUSE - DINING ROOM - AFTERNOON

All four are sitting around the dining room table. Everyone is eating a steak except for Troy who is eating chicken and dumplings.

REBECCA
So, Ronnie how are you liking NCU?

RONNIE
I'm liking it a lot maam. Football is pretty demanding and the classes are pretty tough, but yeah I'm liking it a lot.

CLIFF
So, do you get any kind of special accommodation because you are a football player?

RONNIE
Hardly. I think most the professors treat athletes in general a whole lot tougher so as not to look like there is preferential treatment.

TROY
Yeah he's got one...wow.

RONNIE
Yeah he's pretty bad. Pretty sure he's a closet racist.

TROY
Not so much in the closet. Some of the things Ronnie tells me he says to the class are pretty bad. In fact, Ronnie put him in his place last week and then, Ronnie you tell it.

RONNIE
Not really much to say, but I questioned him on whether or not Admiral Peary was actually first to set foot on the North Pole, and he said I was just sticking up for the black man.

TROY
Then he said Ronnie came from a low-rent-ghetto black high school.

CLIFF
Sounds like this dude is a first-class douche bag.

                         REBECCA
            Cliff!

                         CLIFF
            I mean dish rag. A first-class dish
            rag.

                         TROY
                    (laughing)
            What does that even mean dad?

                         CLIFF
            Well it means he...uh...he...never
            mind I've got nothing.

Troy and Ronnie laugh and Rebecca shakes her head.

                         CLIFF (CONT'D)
            And thanks a lot **son**.

Troy finishes up eating and then pushes back from the table.

                         TROY
            Well we need to head out.

                         CLIFF
            The team watching film tonight?

                         TROY
            You guessed it.

                         RONNIE
            Mrs. Dunn thanks for everything. I
            mean the steaks were fantastic. And
            Mr. Dunn thank you too. You guys
            really know how to make someone feel
            welcome.

Rebecca tears up and gives Ronnie a hug.

                         REBECCA
            You are welcome here anytime Ronnie.

Cliff reaches out and shakes Ronnie's hand as Rebecca releases
her grip on Ronnie and then hugs Troy. The boys pick up their
bags and start walking out the door.

                         CLIFF
            You boys have a safe, trip and we
            will see you next Saturday afternoon.
            Arizona State?

                         TROY
            Arizona State.

The boys walk down the driveway, throw their bags in the trunk of the car, and get inside. Troy starts the engine.

> RONNIE
> (stoically)
> Your mom hugged me first.

> TROY
> I noticed that.

Troy screeches off.

INT. HISTORY BUILDING HALLWAY - MORNING

Ronnie walks down the crowded history building hallway carrying a loaded down backpack. He casually turns left into Professor Billingham's classroom.

INT. BILLINGHAM CLASSROOM - MORNING

A skinny, pale faced teaching assistant with a ponytail is sitting in front of the class reading a book. Ronnie walks across the front of the room towards his seat. Several students whisper as he walks by. Ronnie sits in his seat and starts to unload his backpack. The teaching assistant looks up.

> TEACHING ASSISTANT
> Hold on there Mr. Pippen. No need to unpack.

Ronnie freezes and looks over at the teaching assistant.

> TEACHING ASSISTANT (CONT'D)
> You need to gather all your things and immediately go to Dean Drescoll's office. Room 217.

> RONNIE
> (calmly)
> Why do I need to immediately go to Dean Drescoll's office?

> TEACHING ASSISTANT
> Hey! I was told to call campus police if you gave me any trouble.

Ronnie stands up and starts putting his books in his backpack.

> RONNIE
> Chill out dude--just asking a question.

Ronnie walks back across the front of the classroom toward the door.

                    TEACHING ASSISTANT
                      (under his breath)
                  Cheater cheater pumpkin eater.

Ronnie hesitates then continues out the door.

INT. WAITING ROOM TO DRESCOLL'S OFFICE -- MORNING

The staffer, Sharon Higbee, that helped Ronnie check in to
the dorms is sitting behind a desk writing on a tablet. She
is well dressed and very professional looking.

                          SHARON
                      (on the phone)
                  No problem Dean, I'll let everyone
                  know. Will do. Goodbye.

The door opens and Ronnie enters. He sees Sharon and smiles.

                          RONNIE
                  Hey hey.

                          SHARON
                  Well well Mr. Pippen, nice to see
                  you again but certainly not under
                  these circumstances.

                          RONNIE
                  Under these circumstances?

                          SHARON
                  Yes...under these circumstances.

                          RONNIE
                  I'm sorry, but I really have no idea
                  what is going on or why I was told
                  to come here.

Sharon gazes at Ronnie's face.

                          SHARON
                      (Under her breath)
                  You really don't know.

                          RONNIE
                  I'm sorry?

                          SHARON
                  You really don't know do you?

                          RONNIE
                  I really don't.

Sharon shuffles through some papers and stops to read one.

SHARON
Ronnie I hate to be the one to tell you this but Professor Billingham has accused you of cheating and Dean Drescoll has already drafted the paperwork to expel you from NCU.

RONNIE
What? Cheating? Are you freaking kidding me?

SHARON
He said he found a cheat sheet under your desk.

RONNIE
It's a setup. He didn't like me from day one and now...agh!

SHARON
Well you have a little time to get your story together. Dean Drescoll called right before you walked in the door. He is stuck in a meeting at our south campus and won't be in for another hour and a half or so.

RONNIE
Get my story together? I have no story. I didn't cheat.

SHARON
I'm truly sorry Ronnie.

Ronnie stands up and walks over to Sharon's desk.

RONNIE
I really need to use your phone.

SHARON
I'm not supposed to...

RONNIE
Please I really need your help... again.

SHARON
(smiling)
Make it quick.

Sharon pushes the phone around to Ronnie's side of the desk. He picks up the receiver and dials a number.

                    TROY (O.S.)
          Hello, you've reached the cell phone
          of Troy Dunn. I'm either in class,
          on the field or in the weight room.
          Please leave a message, and I will
          get right back to you.
               (Beep)

                    RONNIE
               (desperately)
          Troy! Billingham has accused me of
          cheating which is total crap. I have
          some sort of meeting in an hour and
          a half or so with him and the Dean
          of Business. I was told they are
          going to kick me out. I'm not sure
          what to do. I need you my friend.

Ronnie hangs up the phone and sits back down.

                    SHARON
          So what are you going to do?

                    RONNIE
          Wait here for the meeting I guess. I
          mean what else can I do?

A concerned look is on Ronnie's face as he looks at numerous plaques and accolades on Dean Drescoll's waiting room wall.

FADE OUT

FADE IN:

INT. WAITING ROOM TO DRESCOLL'S OFFICE -- MORNING

Ronnie is sitting contorted sound asleep in his chair. The outside door opens and DEAN MARCUS DRESCOLL and Professor Billingham come walking in together yucking it up. They both stop when they notice Ronnie sleeping.

                    PROFESSOR BILLINGHAM
               (Shaking his head)
          Lazy. They are all lazy.

Dean Drescoll looks at Billingham with a miffed look on his face.

                    DEAN DRESCOLL
          Sharon, how long has he been here?

                    SHARON
          About two hours Dean.

Billingham smiles.

> DEAN DRESCOLL
> Well, wake him up and send him on into the conference room.

Professor Billingham and Dean Drescoll walk into the conference room.

> PROFESSOR BILLINGHAM
> Let's make this quick Marcus. I have a 3:00 tee time at the club that I really don't want to be late for.

Sharon walks over and slightly gives Ronnie a nudge.

> SHARON
> Wake up Ronnie. They are waiting for you in the conference room.

Ronnie jumps up and rubs his eyes.

> RONNIE
> Man...I sure was hoping this was a dream or nightmare or something.

> SHARON
> This is no dream Ronnie.

Ronnie takes a deep breath and walks into the office.

INT. DEAN DRESCOLL'S CONFERENCE ROOM - AFTERNOON

Dean Drescoll, sitting beside Billingham at a large marble conference table, motions towards one of the 5 empty chairs sitting opposite of where the two academics are currently sitting.

> DEAN DRESCOLL
> Have a seat Mr. Pippen.

Ronnie takes a seat.

> DEAN DRESCOLL (CONT'D)
> Ronnie let's get down to the chase. Professor Billingham has accused you of cheating on a test that you took in his class.

Ronnie jumps up.

> RONNIE
> (interrupting)
> What evidence does he have?!

DEAN DRESCOLL
Ronnie you need to calm down and stay seated.

Ronnie sits down.

RONNIE
(gritting his teeth but calmly)
What evidence does he have?

DEAN DRESCOLL
We'll get to that but first I have to follow procedure and ask you a few questions.

Dean Drescoll opens up a binder and flips through a few pages, pulls out his pen, and begins to write.

DEAN DRESCOLL (CONT'D)
Is your name Ronnie Pippen?

RONNIE
Yes.

DEAN DRESCOLL
Are you a student at Northern California University?

RONNIE
Yes.

DEAN DRESCOLL
On Monday September 10, 2012 did you take a test in Professor Billingham's class?

RONNIE
Yes.

DEAN DRESCOLL
Did you use any outside resources that were not approved to be utilized to aid you in taking this test?

RONNIE
If you are asking me did I cheat, my answer is no!

DEAN DRESCOLL
The problem, Ronnie, is that Professor Billingham has supplied me with a sheet of paper that had many of the answers on the test. He said he found
(MORE)

                        DEAN DRESCOLL (CONT'D)
                    it underneath the desk you were
                    sitting in; and he said it was clearly
                    your handwriting.

Ronnie jumps up again.

                              RONNIE
                    Well Professor Billingham is a bald-
                    faced liar! Let me see the paper!

                         PROFESSOR BILLINGHAM
                    Marcus, do you want me to call
                    security?

                            DEAN DRESCOLL
                    No Lloyd, I don't want you to call
                    security, and Ronnie you must keep
                    seated and control your temper.

                              RONNIE
                    Well, it's hard to control my temper
                    when I am getting accused of doing
                    something I know I didn't do!

                         PROFESSOR BILLINGHAM
                    Enough of this! Just sign the paper
                    and let's get this criminal out of
                    our school!

                              RONNIE
                    Criminal? I have a right to see the
                    evidence if you are going to kick me
                    out!

                            DEAN DRESCOLL
                    That he does.

Dean Drescoll opens up a folder and takes out the piece of
paper with the visible crumpled creases on it. He starts to
hand it across the table to Ronnie when Professor Billingham
jumps up and grabs his arm.

                         PROFESSOR BILLINGHAM
                    Stop! That is the only piece of
                    evidence we have. If we just hand it
                    to him, he could rip it up or sprint
                    out the door with it. Hold it up and
                    let him look at it but not too close.

                              RONNIE
                    You've got to be kidding me.

Dean Drescoll holds up the paper in a very tentatively way.
Ronnie stands up trying to peer at the paper.

                    RONNIE (CONT'D)
          I'll put my hands behind my back if
          it makes you feel better.

                    PROFESSOR BILLINGHAM
          I'm sure you're an expert at that.

Ronnie ignores the comment, puts his hands behind his back
and peers closer to the paper. He falls back in his seat.

                    RONNIE
          That is not my handwriting!

                    PROFESSOR BILLINGHAM
          Oh yes it is! I knew you would try
          to lie your way out of this!

There is a knock on the door, and Sharon sticks her head in.

                    SHARON
          Dean, there are some people here to
          see you.

                    DEAN DRESCOLL
          Do they have an appointment?

                    SHARON
          No but...

                    CLIFF
          Excuse me maam.

Cliff Dunn, DALLAS MONROE a 6'5" 280 pound 52 year old white
male, HADLEE PENNYE a 6'2" 220 pound 38 year old black male,
SANTIAGO JAVIAR BANDERAS a 60 year old Hispanic male, ABBOT
SHUMAKER a good looking 31 year old white male, and ALEXIS
HOPKINS 6' slender, gorgeous white female blonde all well-
dressed caring brief cases in tow walk in and make themselves
at home sitting around the conference table. Cliff remains
standing. Ronnie is speechless. Dean Drescoll looks over at
Professor Billingham who is taken aback by this intrusion
and enormous show of bravado by these intruders. Billingham
jumps up.

                    PROFESSOR BILLINGHAM
               (aggressively)
          What is the meaning of this and how
          dare you interrupt this proceeding?!

                    CLIFF
               (not giving an inch)
          The meaning of this, and I have to
          presume you are Professor
          Billinghauser

                    PROFESSOR BILLINGHAM
          (interrupting) Billingham!

                    CLIFF
          The meaning of this Professor
          BillingHAM is you have accused my
          client, Mr. Pippen, of cheating with
          a threat of expulsion and my partners
          and I think it would not be fair for
          Mr. Pippen to have to defend himself
          without proper representation from
          the law firm that has won more racial
          harassment discrimination cases then
          any firm on the west coast, The Dunn
          Group. So, you need to sit your fat
          butt right back down in that chair
          and show me all the evidence that
          you have that proves my client has
          perpetrated the act that you have
          accused him of.

                    PROFESSOR BILLINGHAM
          I don't have to show you anything!

                    CLIFF
          I was hoping you would say that.

Cliff puts his hand on Ronnie's shoulder.

                    CLIFF (CONT'D)
          Ronnie let's go. You are about to
          become a very wealthy man.

Cliff looks over at Dean Drescoll.

                    CLIFF (CONT'D)
          And I have to assume you are Dean
          Drescoll?

Drescoll nods.

                    CLIFF (CONT'D)
          And you, sir, are about to be
          unemployed.

Cliff looks at the gentlemen he walked in with.

                    CLIFF (CONT'D)
          Let's get out of here.

The gentlemen and lady start moving about. Drescoll stands
up.

                    DEAN DRESCOLL
                (panicked)
            Wait, wait, gentlemen, have a seat.
            Yes, have a seat I am sure we can
            work this all out.

                    PROFESSOR BILLINGHAM
            Dean!

                    DEAN DRESCOLL
            Shut up Lloyd. Now sirs and maam,
            let's just start over again with
            proper introductions.

Dean Drescoll stands up and holds out his hand to Cliff and
Cliff extends his.

                    DEAN DRESCOLL (CONT'D)
            Marcus Drescoll pleased to meet you.

                    CLIFF
            Cliff Dunn.

Dean Drescoll holds out his hand to Dallas and Dallas extends
his.

                    DEAN DRESCOLL
            Marcus Drescoll pleased to meet you.

                    DALLAS
            Dallas Monroe.

Dean Drescoll holds out his hand to Hadlee, and Hadlee extends
his.

                    DEAN DRESCOLL
            Marcus Drescoll pleased to meet you.

                    HADLEE
            Hadlee Pennye.

Dean Drescoll holds out his hand to Parnell and Parnell
extends his.

                    DEAN DRESCOLL
            Marcus Drescoll pleased to meet you.

                    ABBOT
                (British accent) Abbot Shumaker.

Professor Billingham squirms in his chair and rolls his eyes
at the patronizing respect being shown by Drescoll. Dean
Drescoll holds out his hand to Alexis and Alexis extends
hers.

                    DEAN DRESCOLL
          Marcus Drescoll pleased to meet you.

                    ALEXIS
          Alexis Hopkins.

Dean Drescoll holds out his hand to Santiago and Santiago
extends his.

                    DEAN DRESCOLL
          Marcus Drescoll pleased to meet you.

                    SANTIAGO
          (thick Hispanic accent) Santiago
          Javiar Banderas.

Dean Drescoll sits back down and shuffles a small stack of
papers on his desk.

                    DEAN DRESCOLL
          Now gentleman, I am sure your client,
          Mr. Pippen, is normally a very good
          person, but in this case we do have
          evidence of his cheating.

Drescoll looks at Billingham.

                    DEAN DRESCOLL (CONT'D)
          Professor, please present the evidence
          to the gentlemen.

Drescoll looks over at Alexis.

                    DEAN DRESCOLL (CONT'D)
          And gentlewoman.

Professor Billingham reluctantly picks up the note and extends
it to Cliff.

                    CLIFF
          Please place it on the table.

Cliff stands up, puts on his glasses and takes a bird's eye
view of the note.

                    CLIFF (CONT'D)
              (still looking at the
               note)
          Ronnie is this your handwriting?

                    RONNIE
          No sir.

                    CLIFF
          I didn't think so.

He continues to study the note.

                    CLIFF (CONT'D)
          Have you touched this at all?

                    RONNIE
          No sir. Billingham wouldn't let me.
          He said I might run out of the door
          with it.

Immediately Hadlee Pennye springs out of his chair.

                    HADLEE
          He said what?! That you might run
          out the door with it?!

Hadlee turns to Cliff.

                    HADLEE (CONT'D)
          Cliff lets fry this chump. Let's
          just get out of here, draw up the
          lawsuit, and send both of them
          packing.

Turns to Ronnie.

                    HADLEE (CONT'D)
          Ronnie, I will work on this for free.
          Heck, I will pay you to let me work
          on it. We have to make a statement
          that a racist will not be allowed to
          spew his vile and vitriol in a
          taxpayer funded university anywhere
          in California.

Professor Billingham pounds his fist on the table.

                    PROFESSOR BILLINGHAM
          Racist?! Racist?! How dare you!

Dallas whispers to Parnell.

                    DALLAS
              (whisper)
          Another how dare you moment.

They both smile.

Professor Billingham stands up.

                    PROFESSOR BILLINGHAM
          Marcus, I am not going to stay here
          and have my impeccable character
          impugned by these bunch of bullies.

                    DEAN DRESCOLL
          Sit down!

Professor Billingham slowly sits down.

                    CLIFF
          Santiago please procure the note.
          This is the only piece of evidence
          they have, so we need to treat it
          with the utmost care.

Santiago opens his briefcase and pulls out a pair of tweezers
and a plastic baggy. He carefully picks up the note from the
corner and meticulously places it in the baggy. He seals the
baggy and sets it in the briefcase. He then locks the
briefcase.

                    CLIFF (CONT'D)
          Dean, we will be running a restriction
          fragment length polymorphism DNA
          analysis to find out who has touched
          this note. If Ronnie's DNA is not on
          it, which I am sure it is not, you
          are going to have a big problem on
          your hands.

Cliff looks over at Billingham.

                    CLIFF (CONT'D)
          Professor, I have a few questions I
          would like to ask you. I realize you
          have no obligation to answer them,
          but you need to understand if you
          don't, we will leave and immediately
          file a racial discrimination lawsuit
          against you, Dean Drescoll, and this
          university.

                    DEAN DRESCOLL
          Don't worry he will answer the
          questions.

                    CLIFF
          Professor Billingham have you on
          multiple occasions referred to my
          client as boy?

Everyone at the table begin taking notes.

                    PROFESSOR BILLINGHAM
          Yes. I'm sure I have. I see nothing
          wrong with it.

Dean Drescoll drops his head.

CLIFF
Professor Billingham did you refer
to my client as a football player
from a low-rent-ghetto black high
school?

PROFESSOR BILLINGHAM
Yes I did! Is he not?

Dean Drescoll raises his head.

DEAN DRESCOLL
Ok, ok, I've heard enough.

Dean Drescoll looks over at Ronnie and gazes at him for a
moment clearly getting his thoughts together.

DEAN DRESCOLL (CONT'D)
Ronnie, on behalf of Northern
California University and specifically
from me, the Dean of the History
Department, I want to apologize to
you for having to endure this
embarrassment. I find that the only
evidence of any cheating is so tainted
by
    (glares at Billingham)

DEAN DRESCOLL (CONT'D)
blinded, biased, impropriety that I
deem it unreliable. Again, Ronnie I
am truly sorry.

Hadlee springs up.

HADLEE
(screaming)
Do you think some lame apology is
going to undo what this clown has
done to our client?! If I was the
man I was 5 years ago, I'd take a...
    (slams his folder on
    the desk)
FLAMETHROWER to this place.

DEAN DRESCOLL
(wide-eyed and rattled)
No,No I don't think an apology is
enough Mr. Pennye, but what would
you have me do?

HADLEE
(immediately)
Send him packing! Today!

Cliff hand gestures to Handlee to sit down and relax. Handlee sits down.

                    CLIFF
          Dean we do appreciate the gesture,
          but I would like to consult with my
          client about what he thinks the next
          steps should be.

Cliff stands followed by everyone in the room except for Billingham who stays seated with his arms crossed staring at the floor. Cliff extends his hand and Dean Drescoll does the same.

                    CLIFF (CONT'D)
          I will call you this afternoon to
          let you know what we come up with.

Cliff and the entire gang file out of the conference room.

EXT. CAMPUS GROUNDS OUTSIDE OF THE HISTORY BUILDING -- AFTERNOON

Ronnie, Cliff, Hadlee, Dallas, Alexis, Parnell and Santiago walk out of the history building. Ronnie stops.

                    CLIFF
          Just keep walking Ronnie. We will
          talk in the parking lot.

The gang walks about 30 yards into the parking lot. Cliff stops and smiles at Ronnie.

                    RONNIE
          Mr. Dunn, I don't know what to say.
          I mean I can't say thank you enough
          to you...I mean to all of you.

                    ALEXIS
               (thick New York accent)
          No problem Ronnie it was our pleasure.

                    ABBOT
          Yes Ronnie it was actually kind of
          fun. It gave me a chance to work
          on...

Abbot clears his throat.

                    ABBOT (CONT'D)
               (British accent)
          my British accent.

                    SANTIAGO
              (thick Hispanic accent)
          Meester Cliff do we get to keep the
          suits?

Ronnie looks at Cliff with an inquisitive expression.

                    CLIFF
              (smiling)
          I'm sorry Ronnie. Let me introduce
          my entourage.

Cliff makes a hand gesture to Dallas.

                    CLIFF (CONT'D)
          Ronnie this is Dallas Monroe. My old
          college roommate and best man in my
          wedding.

                    RONNIE
          And ya'll practice law together?

                    DALLAS
          Well not exactly.

                    CLIFF
          Well really, not at all.

                    RONNIE
          But...

Cliff makes a hand gesture to Alexis.

                    CLIFF
          Ronnie this is Alexis Hopkins. Mrs.
          Dunn's beautician.

                    ALEXIS
          Oh Cliffy you know I style your hair
          too.

                    DALLAS
          Cute.

Cliff makes a hand gesture to Abbot.

                    CLIFF
          And this is my good friend Abbot
          Schumaker. Aspiring actor slash writer
          slash owner of fifteen McDonald
          franchises across California and
          Nevada.

                    ABBOT
          What can I say? I love Big Macs.

                    CLIFF
          And also known as the most eligible
          bachelor in Orange County.

Abbot smiles and shrugs.

Cliff makes a hand gesture to Hadlee.

                    RONNIE
          Please tell me at least HE is a real
          attorney.

Cliff and Hadlee simultaneously shake their heads.

                    HADLEE
          Nope.

                    CLIFF
          Ronnie, let me introduce to you my
          pastor Reverend Hadlee Pennye.

                    HADLEE
          See you in church this Sunday?

                    RONNIE
               (smiling)
          I'm sure you will but what was the
          flamethrower and if I was the man 5
          years ago stuff?

Cliff shakes his head.

                    HADLEE
          Well Ronnie, I am a big Al Pacino
          fan and I watched *Scent of a Woman*
          just last week and well...it just
          came out!

Cliff makes a hand gesture to Santiago.

                    CLIFF
          And finally Ronnie, it is my pleasure
          to introduce to you the gentleman
          known as the "Yardman to the Stars",
          Santiago Javiar Banderas. He's been
          mine for 5 years but he's been Jack
          Nicholson's for 30.

                    SANTIAGO
          Pleeze to meet jew Ronnie.
               (without pausing)
          Meester Cliff do we get to keep the
          suits?

CLIFF
Yes Santiago its yours.

SANTIAGO
And the briefcases?

CLIFF
(laughing)
Sure.

SANTIAGO
(smiling)
Muy bien muy bien. Muchas gracias Senior Dunn.

CLIFF
De nada Senior Banderas.

Cliff turns to Ronnie.

CLIFF (CONT'D)
You see Ronnie it was a heck of a lot cheaper to buy 5 suits and 5 brief cases then to bring in 5 overpriced attorneys all the way out here to put on a dog and pony show.

RONNIE
(laughing)
That's got to be illegal or something right?

CLIFF
I **never** said these guys were lawyers. They might have presumed it, but I never said it. I'm pretty careful about not lying in situations like that.

RONNIE
What about you saying that your law firm has won more racial harassment discrimination cases then any firm on the west coast? I thought you practiced corporate law.

CLIFF
Uh...well I guess I fudged a little on that one.

HADLEE
Don't worry God will forgive you. He's probably up there still laughing.

                    CLIFF
            I hope so.

                    RONNIE
            So Mr. Dunn what's next?

                    CLIFF
            Well Ronnie that's kind of up to
            you. You can easily have him fired
            or at least a reprimand placed in
            his file. The ball's in your court.

Ronnie looks to the ground for a moment, scratches his chin
and looks up smiling.

                    RONNIE
            I think I have an idea.

FADE IN:

INT. BILLINGHAM CLASSROOM - MORNING

The classroom is packed out and moderately talkative as the
last few students find their way to their seats. Professor
Billingham and Ronnie are not in the classroom. Ted looks
over at Smart Aleck #1 and points to Ronnie's empty seat.

They both smile. The door opens and Professor Billingham
walks in dressed in Ronnie's "lunch lady" uniform complete
with hair net adorned. A mixed array of emotions is seen in
the students' faces ranging from bewilderment to hilarity.
Some of the students cannot hold back and a few short spurts
of laughter are heard. Billingham walks to the front of the
class behind the podium expressionless. He reviews his notes
and then looks up.

                    PROFESSOR BILLINGHAM
                (monotone)
            We will start the day learning about
            the top American restaurateurs. Over
            the years the finest restaurateurs
            did not reach the pinnacle of their
            profession by acquiring a degree
            from a prestigious Ivy league school.
            No...most of the men on this acclaimed
            list cut their teeth by cutting their
            fair share of onions, potatoes and
            carrots behind the scenes as they
            pulled themselves up by the boot
            straps in the kitchen.

INT. HALLWAY OUTSIDE OF BILLINGHAM CLASSROOM - MORNING

Ronnie is standing by the two chairs that are meant for late
arrivals just outside of the doorway of Professor Billingham's

class. He is peering into the class trying not to be seen. Billingham's voice is heard in the background. Ted and Ronnie make eye contact and Ronnie gives him a big smile and a wink. Ted immediately looks down at the floor with a look of astonishment on his face. A hand reaches over and touches Ronnie's shoulder. He immediately whips around and smiles.

                    RONNIE
         Mr. Dunn! What are you doing here?

                    CLIFF
         Just finished up my meeting with
         Dean Drescoll. He's really not that
         bad of a guy. He said he has enrolled
         Professor Billingham in a freshman
         African American studies course just
         as you requested and will personally
         make sure the good professor attends
         every class.

Cliff peers into the class.

                  CLIFF (CONT'D)
         So how is he doing? And why aren't
         you in there?

                    RONNIE
         Aw...I thought it would be a little
         too much on him seeing me stare him
         down and laughing as he parades around
         in my old lunch lady outfit.

                    CLIFF
         Ronnie you are a better man than me
         that's for sure. I would have been
         in there 30 minutes early so I could
         get myself a front row seat with my
         iphone in hand filming every minute
         of it.

Cliff peers over Ronnie's shoulder as they both smile and peek into the classroom as Professor Billingham continues his teaching. Ronnie looks back around at Cliff.

                    RONNIE
         Mr. Dunn I just want to again thank...

                    CLIFF
         (interrupting)
         Ronnie...it's all good. Friends take
         care of each other.

                    RONNIE
         Yes sir I know.

                    CLIFF
          Yeah...I know you do. That's why I'm
          so happy you and Troy are friends.

                    RONNIE
          So we can take care of each other?

                    CLIFF
          Yes sir.

                    RONNIE
               (smiling)
          Don't worry Mr. Dunn. I'll take care
          of your boy.
               (wink)

IMMEDIATE CUT

EXT. VARIOUS FOOTBALL STADIUMS SERIES OF SHOTS - FRESHMAN YEAR

A football is shown soaring through the air for about 30 yards into the end zone. Ronnie soars parallel to the ground and makes a spectacular catch for a touchdown.

A football is shown soaring through the air as Ronnie who is 5 yards ahead of the defender easily runs under it for a touchdown.

Troy is under center on the opponents 1 yard line. He fakes a handoff to the full back and races around the right side and dives into the end zone as he is being heavily pursued by the opponent's defense.

EXT. NCU STADIUM -- AFTERNOON

Cliff and Rebecca are seen in the stands. Rebecca is clapping ferociously, and Cliff is yelling and throwing his fist up in the air.

TITLE CARD: "NCU FINISHES 7-4 AS THE WESTERN PACIFIC CONFERENCE RUNNER UP"

EXT. VARIOUS FOOTBALL STADIUMS SERIES OF SHOTS - SOPHOMORE YEAR

The opposing quarterback is under center and receives the snap. He tosses the ball left to the running back. Paul sheds a block and stuffs the RB in the back field for a loss of 4.

Troy is lined up in shotgun formation.

                    OPPOSING LINEBACKER
               (obnoxiously)
          I'm coming for you Dunn! I'm coming
          for you man! You're about to get
          blown up!

The ball is snapped and Troy drops back in the pocket. The
offensive line drops back to pass block. The loud-mouthed
linebacker blitzes from Troy's blind side. As the protection
is failing Troy rolls right. With a smile on his face the
blitzing linebacker out quicks the left tackle and has a
straight shot at Troy and sprints toward him. Out of nowhere
Louis crosses over and lays a vicious hit on him. Immediately
the linebacker is on his back clearly dazed. Louis
victoriously stands over him.

                    LOUIS
          Kaboom

Troy is under center and receives the snap. He fakes the
hand off to the running back and immediately pitches it to
the slot receiver who takes several steps towards the sideline
then pitches it to Ronnie who is reversing behind him. Ronnie
takes off in the opposite direction crossing up several
defenders who trip over themselves trying to switch
directions. Ronnie turns the corner and gains 30 yards before
being tackled.

INT. GRANDMA'S HOUSE -- AFTERNOON

Grandma is sitting as usual in her rocker and Big Daddy as
usual on the couch as they watch the old RCA. Big Daddy jumps
up and whoops.

                    GRANDMA
               (smiling)
          That's my baby.

TITLE CARD: "NCU FINISHES 8-4 AS THE WESTERN PACIFIC
CONFERENCE CHAMPION"

EXT. VARIOUS FOOTBALL STADIUMS SERIES OF SHOTS - JUNIOR YEAR

Troy is in shotgun formation and receives the snap. Ronnie
runs a 15 yard drag route across the middle of the field in
heavy traffic. Troy passes high to him and as Ronnie leaps
and catches it he is wrecked by the oncoming safety. Ronnie
lays on his back for a few intense seconds and then pops up
and jogs off smiling.

The opposing quarterback is under center and receives the
snap. He fakes a hand off to the tailback and bootlegs to
the left. Paul doesn't bite and creams the quarterback into
the ground.

Troy is under shotgun and receives the snap. He eludes the rush and rolls out right. The receivers are well covered. Troy pump fakes making the closing rusher jump up. Troy then takes off down the field and slides before being hit for a gain of 23 yards.

INT. BUFFALO WILD WINGS -- AFTERNOON

Coach Thompson Is sitting at the bar with a big basket of wings in front of him and surrounded by a herd of rowdy Bearcat fans staring at a big screen. On the screen, Ronnie is seen making a diving catch in the end zone. There is an explosion of cheers and high fives.

> FAN #1
> What a catch!

> FAN #2
> Yeah Pippen is unstoppable!

Coach Thompson sits unemotional but beaming with pride.

TITLE CARD: "NCU FINISHES 10-2 FIRST IN THE WESTERN PACIFIC CONFERENCE AND ROSE BOWL CHAMPION"

SERIES OF SHOTS - SENIOR YEAR

Troy lines up in shotgun formation and receives the snap. Immediately the whole line takes off toward the sideline to block for Ronnie running a bubble screen. Troy passes to Ronnie and he takes off reading the lineman's blocks. Louis puts a nasty cut block on a defender allowing Ronnie to find the open field. Ronnie is then stopped by two safeties after a gain of 30 yards.

The opposing quarterback is under center and receives the snap. He fakes a hand off and steps back in the pocket. As he attempts to throw the ball to his receiver running a dig, Paul swims past his blocker, jumps up, and tips the pass. As the ball flutters toward the ground, Willie sprints 10 yards, dives, intercepts the ball, rolls, and springs up celebrating as his teammates mob him.

The ball is on the opponents 5 yard line. Troy is under center and receives the snap. He immediately runs to the right with his running back on his tail. Troy sees a hole, fakes the pitch, and runs in untouched for a touchdown.

TITLE CARD: "NCU BEGINS SEASON 6-0 THE BEST START IN SCHOOL HISTORY"

INT. LOCKER ROOM - LATE AFTERNOON

Several players including Troy are changing out of their practice uniforms into their street clothes. Coach Griffin walks over to Troy.

                  COACH GRIFFIN
     Troy you know how Coach Westfield
     puts a high priority on his players
     being involved in the community.

                  TROY
     Yes sir.

                  COACH GRIFFIN
     Well tomorrow morning he wants you
     to go to an elementary school in the
     city and do a little song and dance
     on leadership or overcoming life's
     obstacles or whatever you want to
     talk about for an hour.

                  WILLIE
       (laughing)
     Man what kind of life's obstacles
     has he had to overcome?

                  LOUIS
     I heard one time he took a little
     too long in the shower before
     breakfast and had to eat cold oatmeal.

All the players start laughing and pretend to be upset.

                  WILLIE
     Oh the horror of it all!

                  COACH GRIFFIN
     Just stop by my office before you
     leave and I will give you the address.

                  TROY
     Yes sir.

EXT. SMITH SCHOOL FOR THE DEAF - MORNING

Troy pulls up to the school and stops before the marquee which displays Smith School for the Deaf established 1947. The address 1102 South Congress Avenue is located at the bottom of the marque.

                  TROY
     School for the deaf?

He picks up and reads a sticky note with the address 1102 South Congress Avenue handwritten on it.

                    TROY (CONT'D)
          I guess this is the right place.

He tosses the note back in the seat and pulls into a visitor only parking spot. He reaches around and grabs a team autographed football from his back seat, gets out of his car, and briskly walks up to the school.

INT. MAIN OFFICE -- CONTINUOUS

Troy walks up to the counter and is greeted by an elderly female attendance clerk. A nameplate with the name RUBY RAE FERGUSON is stationed on the counter.

                    RUBY RAE
          Good morning.
          How may I assist you?

                    TROY
          Uh...yes. My name is Troy Dunn. I'm
          with the NCU football team. I think
          I am supposed to talk to a class
          this morning.

                    RUBY RAE
          Oh yes. I was told to be looking for
          you.

The clerk points straight ahead.

                    RUBY RAE (CONT'D)
          Just go right back out the door you
          came in and keep walking straight
          down the hall. Ms. Holloman's room
          will be about halfway down to the
          left. Room 122.

                    TROY
          Ok thanks.

Troy turns and starts to walk away.

                    RUBY RAE
          Oh, you need to sign in first and
          get a visitor's badge.

Troy turns back around and walks back towards the counter as the clerk opens the sign in notebook. Troy signs the notebook and is handed a visitor's badge.

                    RUBY RAE (CONT'D)
          Just keep that clipped on while you
          are here and return it before you
          leave.

                    TROY
          Oh ok thanks...now I don't know sign
          language. Is that going to be a
          problem? I mean how do I communicate?

                    RUBY RAE
               (smiling)
          No not a problem. Most of the kids
          have cochlear implants or hearing
          aides which help considerably but
          all the kids are excellent lip
          readers. Smith takes pride on
          preparing these kids for life after
          they graduate and lip reading is a
          top priority. Sadly, however, many
          of the kids don't want to talk audibly
          because they think the hearing world
          will look down on them or even make
          fun of them if they don't pronounce
          words just right.

                    TROY
          Wow I didn't know that. I think
          just the opposite, really, and I am
          sure pretty much everybody I know
          does too. I wholeheartedly admire
          people, especially kids, that have
          to overcome huge life struggles such
          as being hearing impaired.

                    RUBY RAE
          You'd be surprised at all the callused
          jerks out there.
               (stares off into space)
          The things I've been told...um.
               (looks back at Troy)
          I'm sorry...anyway if there is
          something they can't understand,
          Ms. Holloman will sign for you.

                    TROY
          Thank you for your help.

                    RUBY RAE
               (signs and mouths)
          Your welcome.

Troy awkwardly smiles, turns, and walks out the door.

109.

INT. HALLWAY -- CONTINUOUS

Troy slowly walks down the hall and curiously peers in various classrooms as he walks by. One of the teachers, ANGELA REACHER, smiles as he passes her room. He walks up to the open door that has Room 122 Ms. Nicole Holloman clearly printed across the top of. NICOLE HOLLOMAN is at the front of the class with her back to the door enthusiastically teaching a lively bunch of 2nd grade students. He uncomfortably stands at the doorway and lightly raps on the door.

                    TROY
        Excuse me. Ms. Holloman.

Nicole continues her high energy teaching. Troy steps a little closer to the doorway. Several of the students see Troy standing there and point.

INT. HOLLOMAN CLASSROOM -- MORNING

                    DEAF MALE STUDENT #1
          (pointing)
        Ms. Holloman there is someone at the
        door.

Turns around and faces Ronnie.

                    NICOLE
        Oh I'm sorry. Yes can I help...

Troy immediately takes a step back.

                    TROY
          (stuttering))
        You're uh uh uh.

                    NICOLE
        Deaf?

                    TROY
        No...no you're not deaf...you're uh
        uh

                    NICOLE
        Uh yes I am.

                    TROY
          (surprised)
        Oh you are? I'm sorry. I mean not
        like that. I mean I think I saw you
        at Buckaroo Bowl about 4 years ago.
        You left your sweater. I think I
        might still have it.

                    NICOLE
          You have my sweater?

                    TROY
          I tried chasing you down in the
          parking lot to give it back but
          you...wait that explains it. You're
          deaf.

                    NICOLE
          I think that has firmly been
          established.

                    TROY
          I can't believe this...Well I'm here
          to talk to your class about
          leadership. I'm with the NCU football.
          You knew I was coming right?

                    NICOLE
               (smiling)
          Of course. I don't know much about
          sports, but these kids sure do.

Nicole turns to the class.

                    NICOLE (CONT'D)
          Kids we have a visitor. He plays
          football for Northern California
          University. His name is...

Samuel throws a fist in the air.

                    SAMUEL
          Troy "The Gun" Dunn. C'mon Ms.
          Holloman, we all know who he is.

                    DEAF FEMALE STUDENT #1
          I don't know who he is!

                    DEAF MALE STUDENT #2
               (Matter-of-factly)
          Never heard of him.

The students then get into a comical signing argument of who
has and who hasn't heard of him. Troy walks in the classroom
and awkwardly turns his back to the kids and looks at Nicole.

                    TROY
          So how do I do this? Do I just talk
          normal?

                              NICOLE
                    Yes. Just act like this is a hearing
                    class except don't turn your back to
                    them.

                              TROY
                    Like I'm doing now?

                              NICOLE
                    Like you're doing now.

Troy turns around facing the class.

                              SAMUEL
                    So are you through telling secrets?

                              TROY
                         (smiling)
                    Yes I am. What is your name.

                              SAMUEL
                    Samuel Haynes...

                              TROY
                    Well Samuel, I love your
                    straightforward honesty.

Samuel starts grinning.

                              TROY (CONT'D)
                    As a matter of fact, that is one of
                    the characteristics of a good leader,
                    honesty. Just telling the truth even
                    when it might not be to your benefit
                    when you do it. What other qualities
                    do good leaders have?

Hands go up all over the class. Troy points at a cute little
girl on the back row.

                              DEAF FEMALE STUDENT #2
                    Being someone you can depend on!

                              TROY
                    That's exactly right! --just doing
                    what you say you are going to do.
                    It's that simple, yet most people
                    don't do it. My dad taught me a long
                    time ago that I can jump to the top
                    of any group that I'm a part of by
                    just being dependable. Someone that
                    does what he says he's going to do.
                    He calls them 10 percenters because
                    he says 90 percent of the people
                    don't do it.

Samuel raises his hand.

>   SAMUEL
>   Are you a 10 percenter?
>
>   TROY
>   (smiling)
>   I sure try to be.
>
>   SAMUEL
>   Ms. Holloman are you a 10 percenter?
>
>   NICOLE
>   I sure try to be as well. Now Samuel
>   let's let our guest speaker continue
>   teaching us about leadership.
>
>   TROY
>   To be a good leader you have to be
>   committed--committed to your school,
>   committed to your faith, committed
>   to your team. Whatever it is that
>   you are a part of that you want to
>   lead, you have to be committed and
>   dedicated to it.
>
>   DEAF FEMALE STUDENT #3
>   Are you committed to your team?
>
>   TROY
>   Oh yes maam I am. Practice 6 days a
>   week, early morning workouts, team
>   meetings, off season conditioning
>   and of course game day!
>
>   SAMUEL
>   (fist pumps) Game day!
>
>   TROY
>   (laughing)
>   So Samuel you're a pretty big fan
>   are you?
>
>   SAMUEL
>   The biggest!
>
>   TROY
>   Well here's a football autographed
>   by every member of this year's NCU
>   football team.

Troy tosses him the football. He yells and the rest of the class goes ballistic and starts yelling and signing and screaming "no fair" and "why does he get a football?". Troy looks over at Nicole.

                    NICOLE
               (mouths)
          I can't believe you just did that.

                    TROY
          And it's for the entire class, so
          everyone pass it around and then
          give it to Ms. Holloman so she can
          display it...

Troy looks around the classroom.

                    TROY (CONT'D)
          anywhere she wants to.

The kids start passing the ball around. The lights flash
twice.

                    SAMUEL
          Gym time!

Immediately the kids stand up and start putting things away
in their backpacks and then begin to file out the door. Deaf
male student #1 tosses the ball to Nicole.

                    DEAF MALE STUDENT #1
          Nice catch.

                    NICOLE
          Thank you Pete.

Troy and Nicole wait in the classroom as the last kid walks
out the door.

                    NICOLE (CONT'D)
          Well, that was interesting.

                    TROY
          Yeah I kind of messed up giving the
          ball to Samuel. But I tried to save
          it.

                    NICOLE
          No, you did fine. The kids really
          enjoyed it.

                    TROY
          They seemed to...So what is Samuel's
          story? He seems like a really cool
          kid.

                    NICOLE
          Well, he is a handful, but I love
          him to death.

Nicole pauses and gathers her thoughts.

>NICOLE (CONT'D)
> Samuel was like most of these kids, born with a hearing disability but unlike most of these kids, as soon as his father found out, he split and has never been heard from again.

>TROY
>Wow.

Kids for the next period start coming into the room. Nicole slightly grimaces.

>NICOLE
>I am really sorry, but I co-teach a home economics class when my kids go to PE.

>TROY
>Uh...ok. Uh...how about coffee sometime? I really want to hear Samuel's story, and I need to give you back your sweater.

>NICOLE
>Yes, that would be great.

>TROY
>How about today after school? What time do you usually leave?

>NICOLE
>I'm normally gone by 4:30 but I take Samuel to his mom's house about 20 minutes away after school every day, so I can meet you somewhere after that.

>TROY
>The team is watching film today at 3:00 so how about meeting me at the Starbucks on the corner of 23rd and Cheyanne at 5:30?

>NICOLE
>(smiling)
>I will meet you there.

Troy gives her a slight wave and turns to leave. ANGELA walks in the room and smiles as he walks past. She turns and watches him walk towards the door. Troy has to dodge a couple of kids as he walks out the door.

ANGELA
Nice moves.

NICOLE
Really Angela?

ANGELA
Yes really. Who is that hunk-a-muffin? He's cute!

NICOLE
A football player from NCU. He came and talked to the class about leadership.

ANGELA
So did you get his number?

NICOLE
I didn't ask him for his number!

ANGELA
I'm not talking about his cell number. His jersey number on the team.

NICOLE
I have no idea. Why?

ANGELA
I don't know. Ok I was talking about his cell number. I would have gotten it!

NICOLE
I know you would have, but I am not like you.

ANGELA
So, what does that mean?

NICOLE
It means you are brash and confident.

ANGELA
And you're just a shy little wall flower?

NICOLE
Yes, a shy little wall flower that is meeting him for coffee after school.

ANGELA
You dirty diva.

                        NICOLE
              It wasn't like that. He asked me.

                        ANGELA
              You dirty diva with the power to
              enchant and mesmerize the opposite
              sex.

                        NICOLE
              Well my powers need a little work
              because I haven't had a date in over
              2 years!

                        ANGELA
              So this is a date?

                        NICOLE
              No, no, it's just coffee.

                        ANGELA
              Just coffee ok.

Angela walks over to the shelf and starts taking out various pots and pans as the kids settle in their seats. Angela turns around.

                        ANGELA (CONT'D)
              If ya'll set a date, can I be your
              maid of honor?

                        NICOLE
              Stop!

INT. FILM ROOM - AFTERNOON

The entire offensive unit is sitting and taking notes as Coach Westfield is breaking down the film. Troy and Ronnie are sitting beside each other on the second row. Ronnie moves his note pad over where Troy can see it.

                        RONNIE
                   (writing)
              "Where were you all morning?"

Troy writes on his pad.

                        TROY
                   (writing)
              "Do you remember sweater girl?"

                        RONNIE
                   (writing)
              "?"

                    TROY
               (writing)
          "Buckaroo Bowl freshman year"

Ronnie smiles and shakes his head in the affirmative.

                    TROY (CONT'D)
               (writing)
          "I'm meeting her for coffee today!!"

                    RONNIE
               (writing)
          "Are you kidding me?"

Troy smiles and shakes in the negative.

                    RONNIE (CONT'D)
               (writing)
          "CRAZY!!!"

EXT. STARBUCKS - LATE AFTERNOON

Troy is walking across the Starbucks parking lot towards the door talking on his cell phone.

                    TROY
          I have no idea. It could be packed
          away anywhere. Please just try to
          find it. Mom, this is very important.
          Mom I'll tell you later. Mom just
          trust me. I'll tell you later. I've
          got to go. Love you bye.

Troy puts the phone in his pocket, opens the door and walks in.

INT. STARBUCKS - LATE AFTERNOON

Troy looks around, spots Nicole sitting in the corner by herself with two coffees on the table, smiles, and walks over to her. Nicole returns the smile.

                    TROY
          Aww I wanted to buy **you** a coffee.

                    NICOLE
          It's ok. I got here a little early.
          I perceive you as a caramel macchiato
          type of guy, so I just got you one.

Troy sits down, picks up the coffee, "cheers" the cup with Nicole's, and starts to drink.

TROY
Well your perception is right on the money.

NICOLE
I also didn't want you to have to stand in that line.

Nicole points to a very long line of people waiting to order.

TROY
Sounds good to me.

Troy takes another sip.

TROY (CONT'D)
So, tell me about my boy Sam.

NICOLE
Uh...Make sure you call him Samuel. He hates to be called Sam.

TROY
Really? Why is that?

NICOLE
Well that's a part of the story.

Troy sits back with a concerned look on his face.

NICOLE (CONT'D)
Like I was telling you at the school as soon as his dad, Sam Cacciola, found out his newborn son was born with a hearing disability he left the hospital waiting room, got in his car, and took off. That piece of ...ugh...just left Samuel and his mom there at the hospital. He never even went in and saw him. Not even for a moment.

Tears start creeping down her face.

NICOLE (CONT'D)
(Wiping her eyes)
I'm sorry.

TROY
It's ok.

NICOLE
So, Monica, Samuel's mom, has raised him as a single parent ever since. I try to help her out any way I can.

TROY
So Samuel hates being called Sam because it reminds him of his dad?

NICOLE
No. It's because it reminds his mother of his dad. She is such a good mom and it just pains her that Samuel will have to grow up without a father figure in his life. Samuel can just sense this pain in her, and he hates it. Anything that has to do with her ex gets her so emotionally bitter.

TROY
Including his name.

NICOLE
Including his name.

TROY
It just seems so unfair.

NICOLE
Well, it is unfair but nobody ever promised any of us fairness. Everyday I see unfairness. But that unfairness is exactly what creates opportunities for all of us to help each other. We can choose to look the other way and ignore it, or we can roll up our sleeves and get in the game and fight. I choose to fight and that's why I'll do just about anything for Samuel and Monica.

Nicole takes a sip of her coffee.

TROY
Well, tell me a little bit about yourself.

NICOLE
(smiling)
What do you want to know?

TROY
Oh, I don't know. The usual I guess. Where are you from? How long have you been teaching? Your favorite color? Do you have a boyfriend? Do you have any plans for tomorrow night? Just the usual questions.

NICOLE
Oh ok. Well let's see. Modesto where
my parents run a really cool little
diner. 2 years. Blue. No. And uh
let's see...I guess no I don't.

TROY
That kind of gets me excited.

NICOLE
(smiling)
Why does that kind of get you excited?

TROY
Well, I have a good friend that lives
in Modesto so we'll have a new place
to eat when I go visit him.

NICOLE
Yes, that sounds so exciting.

TROY
Seriously though, I would have guessed
you'd be seeing someone.

NICOLE
Why would you have guessed that?

TROY
Well you're smart, funny,
compassionate and well, to be
perfectly honest, drop dead gorgeous.

NICOLE
Yea sure. Actually I've only had 2
guy relationships that I would
consider boyfriends. One hearing,
one not. Neither could deal with the
way I am.

TROY
Even the deaf boyfriend? That doesn't
make any sense.

Nicole stares at him with a confused look on her face.

NICOLE
Oh wait I wasn't talking about my
deafness. Both were ok with that. A
little adjusting here and there but
really no big deal. I was talking
about my views on abstinence. You
see I'm a Christian, and one night
at church, when I was 14 years old,
(MORE)

                    NICOLE (CONT'D)
          I made a purity vow to God to not
          have sex until I was married, and I
          have every intention of keeping that
          promise.

                    TROY
               (smiling)
          I know it's not supposed to work
          this way, but that's the sexiest
          thing any girl has every told me.

                    NICOLE
          Well everybody has his or her own
          views about it. So tell me about
          your ex's or your currents.

                    TROY
          Definitely no currents and the only
          real female relationship that I've
          had was with my high school sweetheart
          for about 3 years. But yeah she kind
          of cheated on me when I came up here
          so yeah. I've dated from time to
          time but nothing serious. I'm just
          too busy with football and school to
          keep a girl happy I guess.

They both take a sip of their coffee.

                    TROY (CONT'D)
          So since you have no plans for
          tomorrow night, do you want to hang
          out?

                    NICOLE
          Sure. Do you just want to meet
          somewhere?

                    TROY
          No way.
               (southern accent)
          My pappy learned me better than that.
               (normal)
          How about you text me your address
          and I'll pick you up at let's
          say...sevenish?

                    NICOLE
               (smiling)
          Sounds good.

Troy stands up.

                    TROY
          I need to head back to the dorms.

Nicole stands up, and they gingerly hug.

                    NICOLE
          I think I'll stay here, finish my
          coffee, and people watch.

                    TROY
          Sounds good. See you tomorrow night.

Troy turns around, walks out the door and begins walking across the parking lot towards his car.

                    TROY (CONT'D)
              (Sighs under his breath)
          Wow.

EXT. BUCKAROO BOWL PARKING LOT - EVENING

Troy's Corvette rapidly turns into an empty spot. He jumps out of the car, jogs over to the passenger door, and opens it. Nicole gets out and the two start walking toward the front entrance. Troy stops, turns around, and points across the parking lot.

                    TROY
          Well that's where it all happened.

                    NICOLE
          My leaving you in a cloud of dust?

                    TROY
          Yes, you leaving me in a cloud of
          dust.

The two laugh and start walking side by side to the front entrance.

INT. BUCKAROO BOWL - EVENING

Troy and Nicole walk up to the front counter where Cashier Joe is working.

                    TROY
          Well I found her!

Cashier Joe looks up from his work.

                    CASHIER JOE
          Sir?

                              TROY
                    You don't remember? Pretty girl,
                    lost sweater, 3 years ago.

                              CASHIER JOE
                    Yea sure Sir. What size shoes can I
                    get for you?

                              TROY
                    Twelve. It took me 3 years of
                    searching but I got her back her
                    sweater.

                              CASHIER JOE
                    That's grand. Maam...shoe size?

                              NICOLE
                    Seven please.

Cashier Joe walks over to the shoe rack, grabs two pairs,
walks back, and sets them on the counter.

                              CASHIER JOE
                    Ok. You guys are on lane 31. You
                    have it for an hour. Go over your
                    time, and I'll charge an additional
                    hour. Make sure you return the shoes
                    in the same condition they are in
                    now. If you spill something on them,
                    clean it off. Here is a coupon for
                    our coke and corn dog special in the
                    snack bar. It ends at 9:00. Any
                    questions?

                              TROY
                    No sir. I believe you just about
                    covered everything.

Troy and Nicole grab the shoes and start walking toward lane
31.

                              CASHIER JOE
                    Maam.

Troy and Nicole keep walking.

                              CASHIER JOE (CONT'D)
                         (louder) Maam.

Troy turns around. Taps Nicole and points to Cashier Joe.

                              CASHIER JOE (CONT'D)
                    Congratulations on your found sweater.

Troy shakes his head.

                    NICOLE
              (smiling)
          Thank you.

INT. CAFETERIA - MORNING

Ronnie and Troy are walking across the cafeteria with trays of finished breakfast in hand.

                    RONNIE
          So are you going to Killa Wings with
          us tonight?

                    TROY
          Man I can't.

                    RONNIE
              (shaking his head)
          The girl?

They both put the trays on the dirty dish carousel and start walking across the cafeteria towards the exit.

                    TROY
          Dude, she's more than just the girl.

                    RONNIE
          I know, but this is like the 5th
          time in 2 weeks yall have gone out.

                    TROY
          Sounds like you're keeping count.
              (smiling)
          Are you getting jealous?

                    RONNIE
          Well, actually I am.

Troy stops walking.

                    TROY
          You've got to be kidding me.

                    RONNIE
          Troy, besides Big Daddy, I've never
          had a friend that I could trust and
          knew, and I mean really knew he would
          be there for me when things got tough.
          You are my best friend, and I just
          don't want to lose that.

                    TROY
          Dude, you are my wingman, and I
          promise no matter what comes of my
                        (MORE)

                    TROY (CONT'D)
          relationship with Nicole, I will
          always have your back and be there
          for you. Our adventure is just getting
          started. I promise.

The two exchange a strong embrace. They release and see
several students staring with quizzical looks on their faces.
The two immediately start walking towards the cafeteria exit
again.

                    TROY (CONT'D)
          You definitely need to find a
          girlfriend.

                    RONNIE
          That I do.

EXT. NICOLE'S APARTMENT -- EVENING

Troy walks up the stairs of a very average looking apartment.
With red roses in hand, he rings the doorbell. Samuel opens
the door. Troy stands there with a confused look on his face.

                    TROY
          Uh...hey Samuel. So what are you
          doing here?

                    SAMUEL
          Ms. Holloman will be out in a minute.
          She is running a little late. My mom
          had an emergency at work, and Ms.
          Holloman had to come get me. I get
          to spend the night!

                    TROY
          You do? Well good for you.

                    SAMUEL
          Come on in. I am supposed to keep
          you company.

Troy walks through the front door.

INT. NICOLE'S LIVING ROOM -- EVENING

Designer crosses collected from her teen years to now cover
a small section of the ivory colored walls in Nicole's quaint
living room. A vase filled with assorted pastel colored
flowers are located on the mantel of her small fireplace. An
abstract painting in lovely light colors on the wall over
the fireplace add a serene distinction to the room. Next to
the fireplace is a white cabinet filled with tiny curios,
mementos, and family pictures. Floral printed pillows adorn
her plush, white couch which faces her TV set. She has a

matching love seat nestled in a quiet corner of the room.
Everything in her living room embellishes her femininity.

                    SAMUEL
          You should put the flowers in a glass
          of water so they don't die.

                    TROY
          They're roses Samuel. Not flowers.

                    SAMUEL
               (confused)
          What's the difference?

                    TROY
          Well...You give flowers to your mother
          and you give roses to your...uh..uh.

                    SAMUEL
          To your who?

                    TROY
          Well to your uh.

                    SAMUEL
          Teacher?

                    TROY
          Yes, your teacher!

                    SAMUEL
          Oh.
               (Pause)
          But Ms. Holloman isn't your teacher.

                    TROY
          No, she is not.

                    SAMUEL
               (smiling)
          But she's mine.

Samuel walks over to Troy and holds his hand out. Troy
reluctantly hands the roses to Samuel. Nicole walks out of
the hallway into the living room. Samuel excitedly runs over
to Nicole.

                    SAMUEL (CONT'D)
          Ms. Holloman look what I have for
          you.

                    NICOLE
          Oh Samuel, they are absolutely
          gorgeous!

Nicole looks up at Troy.

                    NICOLE (CONT'D)
               Red roses are my favorite.

Nicole takes the roses from Samuel.

                    NICOLE (CONT'D)
               Let me get them into some water.

Nicole walks to the kitchen. Samuel turns around and smiles ear to ear at Troy. Nicole comes back out of the kitchen holding a small vase housing the roses. She walks over to the small dinette table and places them in the center of it.

                    NICOLE (CONT'D)
               They will look perfect right here.

Nicole turns around and looks at Troy.

                    NICOLE (CONT'D)
               Monica had a water leak at a building
               she is managing and had to get out
               there to get things cleaned up.

                    TROY
               That's what I hear. So we get to run
               with Samuel tonight. Well I have a
               reservation at Chef Chu's grand
               opening in an hour.

                    SAMUEL
               No! No! I want to go putt putt!

Troy looks over at Nicole and she shrugs her shoulders. Troy walks over to Samuel, picks him up by the shoulders, and raises him up where they are looking eye to eye at each other.

                    TROY
               Well putt putt it is!

EXT. PUTT PUTT GOLF COURSE -- EVENING

Montage Various clips of the three getting excited over shots they make and don't make on the course. Samuel putts one off the foot of a giant and goes in the hole. Nicole putts one that ricochets off of several walls and miraculously goes in the hole. Troy hits one a little too hard, bounces off the course and rolls into a fountain. Samuel sets up on the next hole and is about to putt while Troy and Nicole look on.

                    TROY
               Samuel, do you want a coke?

128.

                    SAMUEL
               (smiling)
          Yes!

                    TROY
          Nicole?

                    NICOLE
          No thanks.

                    TROY
          Hot chocolate? Anything?

                    NICOLE
          No. I'm saving my appetite for that
          delicious microwave pizza in the
          snack bar.

                    TROY
          Well ok. I'll be back before ya'll
          finish the next hole.

Troy briskly walks away, and Samuel strokes his putt as Nicole
looks on. Samuel clinches his fist performing a Tiger Woods
fist pump. Nicole laughs and signs "good shot Tiger". Samuel
signs back "Tiger wishes he was this good". Three teenage
boys are walking by with putter and balls in hand. They stop
and begin laughing as they watch Nicole and Samuel sign to
each other.

                    TEENAGE BOY #1
          Watch this.

Two of the boys stop, and the third walks up behind Nicole
without her seeing him.

                    TEENAGE BOY #1 (CONT'D)
               (softly)
          Hey baby you sure looking fine.

The other two boys shriek with laughter.

                    TEENAGE BOY #1 (CONT'D)
               (softly with sign
                language mockery)
          How about you ditching the brat and
          coming over to my place and I'll
          treat you right!

The other two boys continue laughing hysterically and Teenage
Boy #1 walks around behind Samuel unnoticed by him. Troy
walks around the corner with two drinks in hand.

                        TEENAGE BOY #1 (CONT'D)
                   (softly with sign
                   language mockery)
               Hey retard! There's a snake crawling
               over your foot!

The other two boys continue laughing. Troy's face turns fiery
red. Teenage Boy #1 walks back towards the other two. As he
passes Samuel, he bumps into his shoulder. Samuel turns around
towards Teenage boy #1.

                        SAMUEL
               Excuse me I'm sorry.

Teenage boy #1 keeps walking towards the other two without
slowing down.

                        TEENAGE BOY #1
               No problem retard.

Teenage boy #1 approaches the other two.

                        TEENAGE BOY #2
               Dude, that is just wrong.

                        TEENAGE BOY #1
               Who cares? He can't hear it.

The three start laughing and start walking to the snack bar.
Troy starts walking briskly towards them and then stops.

                        TROY
                   (under his breath)
               Easy Troy. You have a lot to lose if
               you beat the living crap out of these
               punks.

Troy takes a deep breath, turns and starts walking back
towards Nicole and Samuel. Samuel runs over to him.

                        SAMUEL
               I'm hungry let's eat.

                        TROY
               No more golf?

Nicole walks up.

                        SAMUEL
               Pizza!

Troy smiles.

130.

INT. PUTT PUTT SNACK BAR -- EVENING

Troy, Nicole, and Samuel are eating pizza and drinking the cokes in a booth. Nicole and Samuel are sitting next to each other and Troy is across from them. The three teenage boys are sitting in a booth diagonally behind them and an overweight black 16 year old girl with her 10 year old sister is sitting directly behind Nicole and Samuel across from the teenage boys.

                    SAMUEL
          This is really good!

                    NICOLE
               (sarcastically)
          Yes it is. Much better than anything
          Chef Chu could have made.

                    TROY
          I don't think Chef Chu does pizza.

The black girl takes a big bite of pizza.

                    TEENAGE BOY #1
          Dang girl. Ain't nobody gonna try
          and steal your pizza. You can take
          your time.

The black girl hears but ignores him. Troy hones into their conversation. She takes another bite. The three boys start laughing.

                    BLACK TEENAGE GIRL
          Why don't you mind your own business?

                    TEENAGE BOY #1
          Why don't you mix in a salad from
          time to time?

The three boys laugh hysterically.

                    TROY
          How do you sign sorry my bad?

                    NICOLE
          Huh?

                    TROY
          How do you sign sorry my bad?

                    NICOLE
               (Signing)
          Sorry my bad. Why?

TROY
Samuel, do you need a refill?

SAMUEL
No thanks.

TROY
Sure you do.

Troy reaches over grabs Samuel's drink, gets up, and walks over to the front counter. He hands the attendant the drink.

TROY (CONT'D)
I would like a refill on this one.

He then hands him his drink.

TROY (CONT'D)
And I would like to exchange this one for an extra large.

ATTENDANT
Sorry sir but we can't exchange. I'll have to charge you full price.

TROY
That's fine. It's worth it.

The attendant takes the drinks and walks over to the fountain machine. He throws Troy's cup in the trash and grabs an extra large cup from the rack. He fills both cups with ice.

ATTENDANT
What sodas do you want sir?

TROY
It doesn't matter.

The attendant turns around.

ATTENDANT
Sir?

TROY
I mean cokes would be fine.

ATTENDANT
In both?

TROY
That's perfect.

Troy reaches over and grabs a handful of napkins. The attendant fills the cups up and sits them on the counter in front of Troy. He types on the register.

                    ATTENDANT
               That'll be $3.46.

Troy gives him a 10 dollar bill.

                    TROY
               Keep the change.

                    ATTENDANT
               Sorry sir we can't take tips.

                    TROY
               It's not a tip. It's for having to
               mop the floor.

                    ATTENDANT
               Huh?

Troy turns around and walks back towards his table. As he
walks by the teenage boys' he lets out a "whoa!" And then
fakes tripping and falls towards their table releasing the
filled cups onto their table and drenching teenage boy #1.
The three boys screech out and scramble away from the
avalanche of soda.

                    TEENAGE BOY #1
               What the heck?

                    TROY
                 (mockingly signing
                  and speaking)
               I thought I saw a snake crawl over
               your foot.

Troy throws the napkins towards Teenage boy #1.

                    TROY (CONT'D)
                 (signing and speaking)
               My bad.

The three boys freeze with a stunned look on their faces.
Troy turns around, and the black 16 year old girl high fives
him as he walks past. Nicole and Samuel continue eating and
talking to each other unaware of the incident that just
occurred behind them. Troy walks up to the table.

                    TROY (CONT'D)
               Ok, time to go.

                    SAMUEL
               Hey where's my coke?

                        TROY
            Sorry Samuel I spilled it, but I
            hear the Dreamery Creamery has a
            chocolate walnut sundae that's calling
            your name!

                        SAMUEL
            With sprinkles and gummy bears?

                        TROY
            Yes! Of course!

                        SAMUEL
            Then what are we waiting for?

Nicole and Samuel get up from the booth and start walking
towards the exit followed by Troy. In the background the
attendant is mopping up the floor as the three teenage boys
angrily clean themselves up.

EXT. NICOLE'S APARTMENT

Troy, Nicole, and Samuel walk up to Nicole's apartment. Nicole
and Samuel walk hand in hand to her apartment. Troy walks
beside Nicole. They stop, and Nicole pulls her keys out of
her purse and she unlocks the door.

                        NICOLE
            Samuel, go on inside and get ready
            for bed. I'll be in in a minute.

                        SAMUEL
            No, I want to stay out here with you
            guys!

Nicole pushes him in the door.

                        TROY
            Good night Samuel.

                        SAMUEL
            Good night Troy!

Nicole closes the door, turns around, and faces Troy.

                        TROY
            Well, tonight didn't quite turn out
            as I had planned it.

                        NICOLE
            I'm sorry Troy. I just had to take
            Samuel. Monica is by herself. I just
            had to.

TROY
Wait wait that's not where I'm going.
I am glad you brought Samuel. It was
really good for him, and it shows me
what I already knew.

NICOLE
And what is that?

TROY
That I am falling head over heels
for the most selfless person I have
ever met in my life. And that your
love for others shines so brightly
it blinds any perceived disability
you think you might have. And the
more time we spend together, the
more my passion for you grows.

Troy and Nicole embrace and share a passionate kiss.

NICOLE
I love you Troy.

TROY
I love you too.

The two embrace deeply. The door opens, and Samuel sticks his head out.

SAMUEL
I can't find the toothpaste!

Nicole turns.

NICOLE
Ok I'm coming.

She turns back around.

NICOLE (CONT'D)
I need to get in there.

TROY
Ok

Troy shuts the door with his foot and Samuel quickly jerks his head back. Troy gives Nicole a quick kiss on the lips.

TROY (CONT'D)
Good night.

NICOLE
Good night.

Troy turns and walks away.

EXT. VARIOUS FOOTBALL STADIUMS

Cliff, Rebecca, Nicole and Samuel are seen cheering in the stands dressed in NCU Bearcat garb.

SERIES OF SHOTS - DIFFERENT DAYS

Troy is under center and receives the snap. He turns and hands the ball off to the running back who runs right off the hip of Louis who created a big hole by pancaking the right tackle. The running back runs for 12 yards.

> PA ANNOUNCER (O.S.)
> First down NCU Bearcats!

The opposing quarterback is under center and receives the snap. He drops back and throws a short pass to his wide receiver who is greeted by a big hit from Willie for a 7 yard gain.

The opposing quarterback is in shotgun and receives the snap. He steps back into the pocket looking for a receiver and then gets blind-sided by Paul.

Troy is under center and receives the snap. He drops back in the pocket. All the receivers are well covered. He eludes a tackle and scrambles out of the pocket. He beats the LB to the sideline and rushes for a 12 yard gain.

The ball is on the opposing team's 17 yard line. Troy is in shotgun and receives the snap. He rolls out right with a blitzing linebacker trailing him. He sees Ronnie heading to the end zone toward the flag. Troy throws a laser at the flag that Ronnie easily snags for a touchdown.

> PA ANNOUNCER (O.S.) (CONT'D)
> Touchdown Dunn to Pippen!

INT. GRANDMA'S HOUSE

Big Daddy and Grandma are cheering and celebrating as they watch the post game wrap up on her B&W TV. Big Daddy is wearing an NCU cap and Grandma is wearing Ronnie's jersey with Pippen labeled on the back.

> TV ANNOUNCER KEITH GALLAGHER
> Another well played game for the Bearcats!

> TV ANNOUNCER BART HACKETT
> Dunn is performing at such a high level that he is almost unstoppable.

                    TV ANNOUNCER KEITH GALLAGHER
          True but when you have a target like
          Ronnie Pippen that is going to catch
          anything that is remotely thrown in
          his vicinity, it sure makes his job
          a lot easier.

                    TV ANNOUNCER BART HACKETT
          Well said. Well that's going to wrap
          it up for this week's NCU game. Be
          sure and tune in next week as your
          9-0 NCU Bearcats take on the 6-3
          Penn State Nittany Lions. And on
          behalf of myself, Keith Gallagher,
          and Bart Hackett and the NCU
          television network, have a great
          evening.

                    BIG DADDY
          9-0 baby!

Big Daddy raises his hand to high five Grandma.

                    GRANDMA
          Baby? Don't you call me baby!

Big Daddy frowns and lowers his hand. Grandma raises her
hand up.

                    GRANDMA (CONT'D)
          But 9-0 sure is sweet!

Big Daddy high fives her.

                    BIG DADDY
          Yeah!

INT. HOLLOMAN CLASSROOM -- MORNING

Miscellaneous NCU paraphernalia is seen throughout the
classroom. Kids are getting ready for a field day picnic.

                    NICOLE
          Boys and girls let's get packed up
          quickly. We have a full day planned
          at the picnic, and we have several
          very big surprises waiting on you.

The kid's excitement level increases as they grab their
backpacks and start filing out the door. Angela approaches
Nicole.

                    ANGELA
          Mr. Jacobs wants to talk to you before
          you leave. I'll get the kids on the
          bus.

                    NICOLE
          Is everything ok?

                    ANGELA
          I don't know.

Nicole walks down the hall and turns into the waiting area
for Mr. Jacob's office.

INT. WAITING ROOM TO JACOBS' OFFICE -- MORNING

The receptionist is gone, so Nicole walks over to Mr.Jacob's
doorway and stops. He is looking deeply at a stack of papers
on his desk. He looks up over his glasses.

                    MR. JACOBS
          Ms. Holloman. Please come in and
          have a seat.

INT. JACOBS' OFFICE -- MORNING

Nicole walks in and sits uncomfortably in the chair across
from Mr. Jacob's 30 year old desk.

                    MR. JACOBS
          Ms. Holloman I have some very bad
          news. The school has been running at
          a deficit for the last four years
          and it has finally caught up with
          us. We are about a million dollars
          in the red, and our creditors have
          filed liens against most of the
          school's property.

Mr. Jacobs looks back down at the papers, shakes his head,
and looks back up at Nicole.

                    MR. JACOBS (CONT'D)
          The bottom line Nicole is this
          institution will be closing its doors
          at the end of this school year and
          most of if not all of its assets
          will be going up for auction. The
          money raised won't be enough to pay
          off everyone owed, but most will get
          something.

Tears start slowing going down Nicole's cheeks.

                    NICOLE
          But Mr. Jacobs the kids...what about
          the kids?

                    MR. JACOBS
          The kids will either have to find
          another school for the deaf or go to
          a public school.

                    NICOLE
          But there's no school catered for
          the deaf within 300 miles. Families
          will have to move.

                    MR. JACOBS
          Or go to public school.

                    NICOLE
          But these kids are family. They love
          each other.

                    MR. JACOBS
          I'm sorry Ms. Holloman. There's
          nothing that can be done at this
          point.

Mr. Jacobs reaches in his desk and pulls out a Kleenex and
hands it to Nicole. She takes it and dabs her eyes.

                    MR. JACOBS (CONT'D)
          I wanted you to know first because
          of the relationship you have with
          the kids and their parents. They are
          going to need a strong shoulder to
          lean on when we make the announcement.

                    NICOLE
          Which is when?

                    MR. JACOBS
          We are going to let the parents know
          in about a month once everything
          gets finalized. This will give them
          enough time to arrange for other
          education alternatives. It will also
          give our faculty and staff time to
          get their resumes out.

Nicole stands up.

                    NICOLE
          I need to get back to my kids.

Mr. Jacobs stands up.

                              MR. JACOBS
                         I'm truly sorry.

Nicole emotes an insincere smile, turns, and leaves.

EXT. PARK -- MORNING

The kids' bus pulls up and stops in the park. Twenty NCU
football players are there including Troy, Louis, Paul, and
Willie. Fifteen of the players are broken off into three
groups of five on their hands and knees.

                              SAMUEL
                         (pointing)
                    Look the team is here!

The kids stand up and start cheering.

                              DEAF FEMALE STUDENT #1
                         But what are they doing?

Angela stands up and motions for the kids to take a seat.

                              ANGELA
                         Kids take a seat. We are about to be
                         given instructions from a special
                         guest.

The bus door opens, and Paul walks in and stands at the front.
He is decked in complete western attire including a ten-gallon
hat, neckerchief, vest, large belt buckle, boots and spurs.

                              PAUL
                         (western accent)
                    Howdy partners. Are ya'll ready for
                    a crazy, wild, fun filled bronc
                    bustin' day?

All the kids on the bus scream out.

                              PAUL (CONT'D)
                         Well then give me a loud Texas yeehaw!

All the kids scream out yeehaw.

                              PAUL (CONT'D)
                         Well, it sounds like ya'll are ready!
                         Here's how we're gonna do it. For
                         all you guys and gals that want a
                         little tamer ride, just mosey on
                         over to my right where big Ben is
                         heading up the stable, and he'll get
                         you set up. For those who want a
                         wilder ride, just head on over to
                                   (MORE)

                    PAUL (CONT'D)
               the corral right behind me for a
               little down and dirty bronc bustin'.
               But make sure your spurs are fastened
               on tight!

Several of the boys let out a masculine "yea".

                    PAUL (CONT'D)
               Now for those wackos out there, and
               you know who you are,

                    DEAF MALE STUDENT #3
                    (Mouths)
               That's me.

                    PAUL
               that have no fear or regard for your
               life or limb over to my left we have
               some of the most nastiest, atrocious
               and ill-tempered dragons found this
               side of the Pecos.

Several of the boys sign "That's where I'm going".

                    PAUL (CONT'D)
               Ok cowboys and cowgirls lets head on
               out!

Paul turns around and leaves. The kids stand up and start
filing out. As they step off the bus, they start sprinting
to their respective group. The kids in the tame group are
gently placed on the back of a player and slowly taken for a
ride. The kids in the bronco group are put on the backs of
players and bounced around until they fall off. The kids in
the dragon group are put on the shoulders of players. The
players then run around jerking and jumping as the kids hold
on to the players' hair and scream. Troy has deaf female
student #1 on his back in the tame area and walks her over
to where the kids are getting on and off. One of the players
helps her off his back. Troy stands up, and the girl reaches
up to him. Troy picks her up.

                    DEAF FEMALE STUDENT #1
               Thank you Mr. Troy.

The girl gives Troy a big hug.

                    TROY
               It was my pleasure.

Troy sets her down, and she runs off. Troy walks over to
Nicole.

                    TROY (CONT'D)
          Hey babe.

                    NICOLE
          Hey.

Troy looks a little concerned.

                    TROY
          They say the eyes are the window to
          the soul, and if that's true your
          eyes are telling me there's something
          really wrong.

Nicole quickly tears up.

                    NICOLE
          They're closing the school.

                    TROY
          What?

                    NICOLE
          They're closing the school Troy. I
          really don't want to talk about it
          here.

                    TROY
          Well, you're going to have to. What
          do you mean they are closing the
          school?

                    NICOLE
          I had a meeting with Mr. Jacobs right
          before we left. He said we are just
          in too much debt.

                    TROY
          What? I mean temporarily?

                    NICOLE
          No Troy. It's permanent. He said
          they are going to auction off all
          they can, and that won't even be
          enough to pay off everybody.

                    TROY
          There's got to be another way around
          this. What about the kids?

                    NICOLE
          He said they will either have to
          find another school for the deaf or
          enroll in public school.

                    TROY
               (Under his breath)
          Samuel.

Tears start streaming down Nicole's face.

                    NICOLE
          Troy, I can't be this way here. I
          have to keep it together.

Samuel is sitting on the shoulders of Willie with both arms
and clinched fists up in the air. Willie races up to Troy
and Nicole.

                    SAMUEL
               (screaming)
          No one can stop Samuel the dragon
          slayer!

                    TROY
          Oh yeah?

Troy reaches up and tickles Samuel on his exposed sides.
Samuel falls back into Troy's arms. Troy swings Him around
and places him on the ground.

                    SAMUEL
          Hey that's not fair!

                    TROY
          Not fair? There are no rules in war!
               (announcing)
          Hear ye hear ye! On this day Samuel
          the dragon slayer has been bested by
          Troy the tickle monster!

                    SAMUEL
          Oh yea?

Samuel races up to Troy and jumps up in his arms. Troy
squeezes him and lets out a roar. Samuel then lets out his
own roar, and Troy falls to the ground. Samuel sits on Troy's
chest and starts playfully pounding him with his fists.

                    TROY
               (laughing)
          Ok, ok, you win! I give up!

Samuel jumps off Troy's chest and runs over to Willie.

                    SAMUEL
          Pick me up dragon. We're off to a
          new adventure.

                    WILLIE
          Your wish is my command.

                    SAMUEL
          Hey dragons can't talk.

                    WILLIE
          Oops sorry. I mean roooooar!

Willie picks him up and puts him on his shoulders then takes off running back to where all the other kids are playing.

                    TROY
          I love that kid. He is so stinking
          cute.

                    NICOLE
          I know. I love Samuel as if he were
          my own.

                    TROY
          Samuel? Oh yea he's cute too.

                    NICOLE
               (looking confused)
          Huh?...Wait.

Nicole picks up a stick lying beside her and throws it at Troy.

                    NICOLE
          Troy this is serious. I don't know
          what to do.

Troy walks over to Nicole and puts his arms around her.

                    TROY
          I don't know what to do either but
          you need to be strong for the kids.

Troy wipes a tear from her eye.

                    TROY (CONT'D)
          And I promise I will be by your side
          fighting for those kids every step
          of the way.

The two embrace.

The camera pans back showing a row of bushes about 15 feet away. Under the bushes four male students are crouched watching Troy and Nicole embrace. They are all smiling and giggling.

EXT. VARIOUS FOOTBALL STADIUMS SERIES OF SHOTS - DIFFERENT DAYS

Troy is under center and receives the snap. He drops back then fires a rocket to Ronnie who is crossing over the middle. Ronnie catches the ball and runs for 8 yards and is brought down for a 25 yard gain.

The opposing quarterback is under center and receives the snap. He hands the ball off to his running back and gets blown up by Willie at the line of scrimmage for no gain.

The ball is on the opposing team's goal line and both teams have their big boys stacking the line of scrimmage. Troy gets the snap and immediately ducks behind and follows Louis who has pushed the nose guard 2 yards into the end zone for a touchdown.

> TV ANNOUNCER KEITH GALLAGHER
> 12-0 Bart. 12-0. I've been broadcasting Bearcat football for 27 years now and that's the first time those words have ever left my mouth.

> TV ANNOUNCER BART HACKETT
> As great as that is Keith there are two other words that surpass them. National Champions.

> TV ANNOUNCER KEITH GALLAGHER
> Oh I so agree. And hopefully in about 30 days, we will be dancing in the streets of Sacramento finishing the season 13-0 and waving a National Championship banner.

EXT. PRACTICE FIELD -- AFTERNOON SERIES OF SHOTS - DIFFERENT DAYS

A montage of shots is shown of the team outfitted in practice gear.

A full offense and defense are on the field, the ball is snapped, Troy drops back and hits Ronnie on a 10 yard out.

A full offense and defense are on the field, and the ball is snapped. Troy pitches to the running back who sweeps around the left side, cuts back in, and is tackled by Willie.

The punting and punt return team is lined up on the field.

The ball is snapped, and the punter punts a high 45 yard punt and is received by the punt returner who is immediately swarmed tackled. The tacklers jump up and start whooping and hollering.

145.

Troy is under center and takes the snap. He pitches the ball left to his tailback who starts to run but then pulls up to pass. Ronnie is open 30 yards down the field. The tailback floats the ball down the field, and Ronnie runs under it, catches the ball, and sprints the remaining 40 yards to the end zone. All the team sans the defensive players that were on the play sprint over to Ronnie. They all start yelling and jumping on each other as pandemonium breaks loose.

The camera pans back to exemplify the excitement.

INT. DORM ROOM -- EVENING

Troy and Ronnie are both lying on their bunks starring at the ceiling.

                TROY
    So this is it.

              RONNIE
    Yea this is it...in less than 24
    hours we will be playing for the
    national championship.

               TROY
    I'm not talking about that man. I
    mean it's the last game you and I
    will ever play together.

              RONNIE
    You don't know that for a fact. We
    both could wind up playing for the
    same NFL team...Have some faith man.

                TROY
    C'mon Ronnie the odds of that
    happening are so remote. Seriously,
    does that not get to you at all?

              RONNIE
    Of course it does. I have even thought
    of somehow putting out on the street
    that whoever drafts me needs to draft
    you. And if they do I will sign for
    less money.

Troy immediately jumps out of his bunk, steps over and cowers over Ronnie, and puts his finger in his face.

                TROY
       (clinched teeth)
    Ronnie DiAngelo Pippen! That is the
    stupidest thing that has ever come
    out of your mouth!
              (MORE)

TROY (CONT'D)
Listen to me Ronnie. You have to promise me you will never try and set up some sort of package deal!

RONNIE
Dang, Troy chill!

TROY
I'm not going to chill until you promise to me you won't do anything so insanely dumb as that!

RONNIE
Ok I promise.

TROY
I'm serious Ronnie.

RONNIE
Troy, I said I promise...dang.

Troy sits down on his bed, and Ronnie sits up.

TROY
Listen man I appreciate the gesture, I really do. But you are a top 5 first round pick and what comes with that is intense scrutiny from any team that is willing to shell out major bucks to get you. If even one team thinks you are going to be a signing problem, they all will run, and it could cost you hundreds of thousands of dollars.

RONNIE
All right man. We'll put it in God's hands then.

TROY
Couldn't think of a better place to be.

Troy lays back down.

RONNIE
Troy.

TROY
Yea?

RONNIE
I just want to say thanks.

Troy sits back up.

> TROY
> For what?

> RONNIE
> For always having my back.

> TROY
> Ronnie you don't have to...

> RONNIE
> (interrupting)
> Yes Troy I do. When I got on that bus to come here, I was scared. I really was. I didn't want Grandma to see it, so I held it in, but I think she knew. The first letter I got from her she said she stayed up till 4:00 the next morning after I left praying that God would place people of character and integrity in my immediate life and that I would find someone I could lean on when times get rough. I knew I could hold my own on the field, but off of it I figured I would just be a loner and would have to fight to be accepted because of what school I was coming from. Troy you always were there for me. I mean from day one. You didn't care about which side of the tracks I was from, and you always treated me with respect. I don't think I could have done this without you.

> TROY
> Ronnie, yes you could have done this without me. It just wouldn't have been as fun.

> RONNIE
> I love you my brother.

Troy stands up and then Ronnie stands up and the two embrace in the middle of the room.

> TROY
> I love you too...my brother.

TITLE CARD: "JANUARY 9, 2012 NEW ORLEANS SUPERDOME BCS NATIONAL CHAMPIONSHIP GAME NORTHERN CALIFORNIAN UNIVERSITY BEARCATS VS UNIVERSITY OF ALABAMA CRIMSON TIDE"

INT. NEW ORLEANS SUPERDOME LOCKER ROOM

Coach Westfield is standing up with his right pointer finger held high in the air. The players, some standing some kneeling, are in a horseshoe around him. He looks at every single player, coach, trainer, and manager in the room dead in the eye, and in a soft but stern voice says, "you have one shot". As he addresses the last player that is behind him, he turns around and faces the front.

>   COACH WESTFIELD
>   (soft but stern)
>   I have one shot.
>   (Loud and methodically)
>   We all have one shot!

The room is silent.

>   COACH WESTFIELD (CONT'D)
>   (normal voice)
>   We all have one shot to win a National
>   Championship. We all have one shot
>   to wear the victor's crown.
>   (pause)
>   There are over 12,000 Division I
>   college football players that would
>   do anything to trade places with you
>   right now. 12,000!

Coach Westfield looks over at several of his coaches that are standing beside each other in the back of the room.

>   COACH WESTFIELD (CONT'D)
>   There are over 5,000 Division I
>   assistant coaches, managers, and
>   trainers that would do anything to
>   be standing in this room right now.

Coach Westfield pauses and looks around the room letting the vibe sink in.

>   COACH WESTFIELD (CONT'D)
>   There are 120 Division I head football
>   coaches that pray every single night
>   for the opportunity to give this
>   pregame national championship speech.
>   I am so blessed. You are so blessed.
>   (pause)
>   We have one shot.
>   (MORE)

COACH WESTFIELD (CONT'D)
(pause)
When we run out on to that field you will hear the roar of 10s of thousands of screaming fans that live and breath Bearcat football. Any fear you have will be silenced by the power of the glory and love that will be filling this stadium for this team. Make no mistake about it you won't just be fighting for us, but you will be laying it all out every single play for them as well.
(pause)
We have a daunting task gentlemen. A daunting task.
(pause)
Alabama has the number one ranked defense in the country, and Levar Presley is one of the best running backs I have ever coached against.
(pause)
And as you know, most of the sports pundits don't think we have much of a chance.
(pause)
But they don't know.
(pause)
BUT THEY DON'T KNOW!
(loudly)

LOUIS
Preach on Coach!

COACH WESTFIELD
But they don't know you like I do. Almost every player here has overcome enormous obstacles to get to this place. And those that haven't have the character to appreciate what others have gone through and are truly aware of how fortunate they are. BUT THEY DON'T KNOW!
They don't know all the sacrifices you made to get where you are today. School, relationships, and even family have all been strained to the point of breaking because of this commitment. BUT THEY DON'T KNOW!

There is an echoing of "THEY DON'T KNOW" from several of the players.

                    COACH WESTFIELD (CONT'D)
               They don't know the love the coaches
               have for you guys and all the hours
               and hours spent studying and planning
               to prepare you to be successful in
               this contest. BUT THEY DON'T KNOW!

There is an echoing of "THEY DON'T KNOW" from several of the
players.

                    COACH WESTFIELD (CONT'D)
               Most importantly they don't know the
               love you guys have for each other
               and what you are willing to do to
               protect and exalt each other at the
               expense of your own adulation if
               that means a victory for this team.
                    (pause)

                    COACH WESTFIELD (CONT'D)
               You guys are truly brothers. And
               because of that love and bond, you
               have out-worked, out-thought, out-
               hustled, out-disciplined and out-
               hearted every team we have faced
               this year, and this game will be no
               different. You are the best football
               team in the stadium and after this
               game, you will show the world you
               are the best college football team
               in the country! YOU WILL NOT BE
               DEFEATED!

                         WILLIE
                    (screaming)
               WE WILL NEVER BE DEFEATED!

The team breaks into pandemonium, and after a few seconds of
yelling and jumping, Coach Griffin opens the side door.

                         COACH GRIFFIN
                    (yelling)
               LET'S DO THIS THING BOYS!

The team bursts out of the locker room into the tunnel.

INT. NEW ORLEANS SUPERDOME

                         PA ANNOUNCER (O.S.)
               Ladies and gentlemen. The Northern
               California Bobcats!

The team sprints out of the tunnel onto the field. INT. NEW
ORLEANS SUPERDOME

SERIES OF SHOTS - DIFFERENT PLAYS

The Alabama quarterback is under center. He takes the snap and pitches left to Presley who turns the corner for a 35 yard gain.

The Alabama quarterback is under center. He takes the snap and drops back looking down the field. He hands the ball off to Presley on a draw play. Presley makes several jukes and cuts and scampers 40 yards for a touchdown.

Troy is in the shotgun. He gets the snap and hits Ronnie going across the middle. Ronnie gets racked but gets up relatively quickly for a 30 yard gain.

Troy is in the shotgun. He gets the snap, bounces, and looks down field. He then starts running down the middle of the field on a quarterback draw. He dives 3 yards from the end zone, gets hit, flips, and lands in for a touchdown.

Troy is in the shotgun. He gets the snap and drops back in the pocket. A blitzing linebacker closes in on him. Troy pump fakes, but the linebacker does not bite and puts his helmet into Troy's chest and knocks him to the ground as a 300 pound defensive lineman lands on top of him.

Troy is under center and takes the snap. He pitches the ball left to his tailback who starts to run but then pulls up to pass. Ronnie is wide open 40 yards down the field with his hand up. As he is about to pass, he gets hit and fumbles the ball. An Alabama cornerback scoops the ball up and runs 70 yards for a touchdown.

Troy is in the shotgun. He gets the snap, bounces, and looks down field. He hits Ronnie running a post pattern 60 yards down the field for a touchdown.

The Alabama quarterback is in the shotgun. He gets the snap and throws left to Presley running a bubble screen. He makes several jukes and cuts and runs 55 yards for a touchdown.

The Alabama quarterback is under center. He takes the snap and drops back in the pocket and flips a pass out to his running back who is immediately tackled by Paul behind the line of scrimmage for a 3 yard loss.

      CHRIS BERMAN
   Well Jon, NCU is certainly fighting
   to the end but Alabama can put the
   game away right here. The Bearcats
   have only one time out left so with
   a first down, they can easily run
   out the clock and The University of
   Alabama would be the new national
   champion.

The Alabama quarterback is in the shotgun. He drops back and fires the ball 15 yards down the field. The ball deflects off the jumping receiver's fingertips and right into the arms of Willie who runs 8 yards down the field and is then tackled. He gets up holding the ball high and runs to the sideline screaming.

                    JON GRUDEN
        What a turn of events! The Bearcats
        still have quite a bit of work to do
        in a short amount of time but what
        ever happens, this has been one heck
        of a game!

                    CHRIS BERMAN
    Agreed.

TITLE CARD: "ALABAMA 35 NORTHERN CALIFORNIA 31 :47 4RTH QUARTER 1ST AND 10 ON THE BEARCAT 37 YARD LINE."

Troy is in the shotgun. He takes the snap and rolls right. He hits Ronnie doing a 15 yard out. Ronnie is immediately pushed out of bounds stopping the clock.

Troy is in the shotgun. He takes the snap and rolls left. Ronnie is running another 15 yard out but on the left side. Troy pump fakes to Ronnie, sets up, and hits his wide open tight end who rumbles for 31 yards and is tackled on the Alabama 17 yard line. The entire team sprints to the line of scrimmage lines up with Troy under center. Troy takes the snap and immediately spikes the ball stopping the clock with 22 seconds showing.

The team stays at the line of scrimmage.

                    CHRIS BERMAN
        Wow, the Bearcats are going no huddle
        to keep Alabama from making any
        substitutions.

Troy lines up in the shotgun and barks out B52 blue B52 blue Argentina Argentina hup. The ball is snapped, and a blitzing linebacker immediately sacks Troy on the 24 yard line as the back of his helmet violently crashes against the turf. On his back, Troy signals for a timeout. The head referee waves his arms signaling a time out with 14 seconds showing on the clock.

                    JON GRUDEN
        Well that no huddle strategy backfired
        in a big way.

                    CHRIS BERMAN
        It was a risk.

JON GRUDEN
Yes a very costly one.

CHRIS BERMAN
Dunn looked a little dazed going over to the sidelines.

JON GRUDEN
(sarcastically)
I wonder why?

CHRIS BERMAN
You think getting smashed to the ground by one of the hardest hitting linebackers in the country had something to do with it?

JON GRUDEN
I'm not a betting man Chris but if I were, I'd bet the house on it.

Troy runs over to the huddle from the sidelines where he was talking to the head coach. The team breaks and trots over to the line of scrimmage. Troy sets up under center and takes the snap. He looks left and then right and sees Ronnie with a half step on the defender. He steps up in the pocket and throws the ball down field into the end zone. Ronnie jumps up with his arms and hands stretching out as far as humanly possible. The ball tips off of his hands into the chest of a defender who muffs it as another defender dives towards the sinking ball which hits the ground and harmlessly bounces away. An official runs over and waves his arms indicating an incomplete pass. Eight seconds is shown left on the clock.

The Bearcat players immediately sprint back and huddle up. A player runs into the huddle from the sideline.

PLAYER
Base spread rose 40 fade.

TROY
(louder)
Base spread rose 40 fade.

RONNIE
Troy are you ok man?

TROY
A little foggy, but I'm good. Don't worry about me.

Ronnie taps his pointer finger on Troy's chest.

                              RONNIE
                    Ok Gun, let's show'em what's inside.
                    Just put it up close. I'll get it.

Troy nods.

                              TROY
                    On 2 on 2.

The team breaks the huddle and gets into formation. Troy
barks out his cadence. The ball is snapped. Troy rolls right
and is met by a blitzing linebacker sailing through the B
gap. Troy side steps, averts the tackle, spins, and scrambles
left. A fallen defensive tackle reaches up and desperately
grabs his foot which Troy shakes off and continues to roll
left. Another blitzing linebacker bears in on him 3 yards
away. Troy pump fakes, the linebacker jumps, and Troy ducks
under his reaching grasp. Troy moves back right as the
pressure of several lineman entrap him. He immediately steps
up and throws a fade to the left back corner of the end zone.
As Troy finishes his follow through his right knee is crushed
by a vicious tackle by a 275 pound defensive lineman. As the
game clock ticks to zero, Ronnie leaps up, reaches behind
his head, and with one hand snags the pass as he comes
crashing down landing with his right heel clearly inside the
back line of the end zone. The back judge signals a touchdown
and pandemonium ensues as the Bearcat players start
celebrating their National Championship victory. Ronnie is
mobbed and buried under a sea of teammates. He scrambles to
get up, and when he does, he gives Louis a hug.

                              RONNIE
                    Nice blocking big man.

Louis lets out a triumphant yell then dives into another dog
pile.

RONNIE'S POV: Several Bearcat players and coaches are standing
around the 20 yard line as a stretcher cart pulls up.

Ronnie runs over to the cart as the attendants are lifting
Troy on to it.

                              RONNIE (CONT'D)
                         (Teary eyed)
                    Troy.

                              TROY
                         (smiling)
                    Don't worry, I'll be fine. What a
                    throw eh?

                              RONNIE
                         (smiling)
                    What a throw? What a catch!

                    TROY
          Yeah, that was pretty good too.

                    RONNIE
          We did it man.

                    TROY
          Yes we did.

                    RONNIE
          Sure you gonna be ok?

                    TROY
          Yeah man. They're taking me to the
          hospital for some x-rays, but I'll
          be all good. Go celebrate!

                    RONNIE
          All right Troy, I'll see you in a
          bit.

As Troy is lying on the cart, they fist bump and Ronnie runs
off to the mass celebration on the field.

INT. HOSPITAL WAITING ROOM -- EVENING

Cliff is standing and occasionally aimlessly pacing as Rebecca
and Nicole sit holding hands with each other. The double
door opens, and DR.BURGESON, a 55 year old orthodedic surgeon,
walks in. Cliff walks over to him. Rebecca and Nicole stand
and walk over as well still holding hands. Dr.Burgeson extends
his hand to Cliff, and he shakes it.

                    DR. BURGESON
          I'm Dr. Burgeson.

                    CLIFF
          Cliff Dunn.

                    DR. BURGESON
          We did several x-rays and an MRI of
          Troy's knee. And of course because
          of the swelling, I can't be definitive
          of the severity of the damage, but
          what is clear is that Troy suffered
          a multiligamentous injury with
          probable concomitant vascular damage.

                    CLIFF
          English doc...please.

                    DR. BURGESON
          Troy tore three ligaments. His acl,
          mcl and cpl. It had to be a
                    (MORE)

DR. BURGESON (CONT'D)
significant blow to do this much damage.

CLIFF
So what exactly is the prognosis? How long will he be down for?

DR. BURGESON
Typically this type of injury will require multiple surgeries and at least 9 to 12 months of rehab. And depending on how well Troy responds to the rehab, he should expect to have about 90% movement of that knee in about 15 months. However, there's a chance he will always have a slight limp.

CLIFF
What about football?

DR. BURGESON
I'm sad to say Mr. Dunn, but realistically Troy's football playing days are over.

REBECCA
He's going to be devastated.

NICOLE
But he will be able to walk on his own right?

DR. BURGESON
Yes there is only a small chance he will even have a noticeable limp.

CLIFF
Did you check for a concussion? I know he seemed a little off on the ride out here.

DR. BURGESON
Yes, we did and have confirmed Troy has a grade 2 concussion. In fact, he told me the team flies back later tonight, but I am not comfortable releasing him to get on a 4 hour red eye back to LA, so I recommend admittance and an overnight stay here for observation and rest. After a good night's sleep and if no further complications, he can be released late morning or early afternoon.

                    CLIFF
          I agree doc. I am sure we can get a
          flight out tomorrow.

                    REBECCA
          When can we see him?

                    DR. BURGESON
          You can go in now.

Dr. Burgeson turns and leaves the room. Ronnie walks into
the waiting room broadly smiling and holding a big trophy.
Engraved on the trophy is BCS National Championship 2012
MVP.

                    REBECCA
          Ronnie!

                    CLIFF
          MVP? Congratulations Ronnie. You
          deserved it. Troy will be so excited
          for you.

                    RONNIE
          You don't know?

                    CLIFF
          I guess not.

                    RONNIE
          The BCS Bowl committee members were
          split who should get it, so they
          gave it to both me and Troy as co-
          MVPs.

                    CLIFF
          Wow.

                    RONNIE
          They only had one trophy so they
          said they would send Troy one...How's
          my boy doing?

Rebecca starts to cry.

                    RONNIE (CONT'D)
               (under his breath)
          No.

                    CLIFF
          Ronnie the doctor said that
          realistically Troy has played in his
          last football game.

A tear rolls down Ronnie's face.

                    RONNIE
          No.

Cliff puts his hand on Ronnie's shoulder.

                    CLIFF
          If this is truly his last game, I
          couldn't imagine a better way to go
          out. National championship and co-
          MVP with his best friend.

                    REBECCA
          Cliff we need to go see him.

Nicole walks over and gives Ronnie a hug.

                    NICOLE
          I am so glad you are here. Troy is
          going to need you.

<The next scene is shot through the window of Troy's room.>
Cliff, Rebecca, Nicole and Ronnie are all surrounding Troy's
bed. Troy has his arm around Nicole as she lays beside him.
Rebecca is holding his hand. Cliff is standing off looking
on. Ronnie is at the foot of the bed with his hand on Troy's
good leg. All are crying or teary eyed. Cliff moves in and
grabs Ronnie's hand and then Rebecca's. Rebecca drops Troy's
hand and grabs Nicole's. Troy continues with his arm around
Nicole and reaches up his other hand to Ronnie, and he grabs
it. Cliff prays for about 20 seconds, and they all embrace
in a group hug.

EXT. HOSPITAL - MORNING

The automatic doors slide open and Troy, sitting in a
wheelchair holding a set of crutches in his lap, gets wheeled
out by a nurse followed by Cliff. A taxi pulls up to the
curb, the trunk pops up, and the driver begins to load the
luggage while Cliff and the nurse help Troy into the car.

INT. TAXI - MORNING

                    CAB DRIVER
              (Thick Cajun accent)
          Where to boss?

                    CLIFF
          The airport. We have a flight to
          Oakland that leaves in 3 hours.

                    CAB DRIVER
          You got it boss.

                    TROY
          Mom and Nicole make it home ok last
          night?

                    CLIFF
          Yes. They said it was a smooth flight.
          It's a shame Nicole couldn't have
          taken a day off so they could have
          stayed over.

                    TROY
          Yes. She's so devoted to those kids...
          Mom picking us up at the airport?

                    CLIFF
          No. Paul told mom to sleep in because
          he wanted to pick us up.

                    TROY
          Paul? No dad.

                    CLIFF
          What's wrong with Paul? He really
          wanted to see how you were doing so
          he is driving all the way from the
          school to pick you up. I thought you
          were boys.

                    TROY
          We are. I love him to death, but I'm
          not excited about listening to "Your
          Cheating Heart" for an hour.

                    CLIFF
               (chuckling)
          How do you not like Hank?

About 10 seconds of silence pass.

                    TROY
          Dad, I just don't get it. I know we
          are not supposed to doubt the
          providence of God, and I know He has
          a plan for my life, but I was just
          so sure football was it. I was just
          so sure.

                    CLIFF
          You're right son. I did too. But I
          am sure He has even bigger plans
          than that for you. You just have to
          trust Him.

                              TROY
                    I know that's what you've taught me,
                    but it's just so hard sometimes.

Troy lets out a sigh.

                              TROY (CONT'D)
                    I really don't feel law school dad.
                    You ok with me not going?

                              CLIFF
                    Son, this is your life, not mine.
                    You do what you have to do, and you
                    know your mom and I will support
                    you.

                              TROY
                    Thanks dad. I guess I'll get a job
                    in the corporate world and put my
                    business degree to work.

                              CLIFF
                    Sounds like a plan son. You are going
                    to be the bomb in whatever you do.

                              TROY
                        (smiling)
                    The bomb dad?

                              CLIFF
                    The bomb!

EXT. DUNN HOUSE - MORNING

Paul's truck pulls up in front of the house in their circle
drive and parks. All three get out of the truck and walk to
the front door with Troy on crutches.

INT. DUNN HOUSE - MORNING

As Troy walks in, he sees a room filled with his teammates,
coaches, the kids from the school, some of the attorneys
from Cliff's firm, and his family and friends.

                              EVERYONE
                    Welcome home!

The kids run up to Troy and start hugging him. Troy puts the
crutches aside and returns the hugs. Nicole wades her way in
through the kids and gives Troy a kiss.

                              TROY
                    Do they know I can't play anymore?

                    NICOLE
          They don't care about that.

                    SAMUEL
          You scared me Troy. Are you ok?

                    TROY
          Oh yes! Nothing can keep Troy the
          tickle monster down!

Samuel jumps up into Troy's arms, and they embrace. Monica
walks over to Troy with Abbot by her side.

                    MONICA
          So we finally get to meet. I'm
          Monica...Samuel's mom.

Troy leans in and gives her a gentle hug.

                    TROY
          I feel like I know you already. I
          have heard so much about you from
          Nicole and Samuel.

                    MONICA
          Trust me, I can say the same about
          you.

Abbot steps up and shakes Troy's hand as Monica stands very
close.

                    ABBOT
          Hey Troy.

Nicole wiggles her finger back and forth at Abbot and Monica.

                    NICOLE
          So do ya'll know each other?

                    MONICA/ABBOT
               (Simultaneously)
          Yes.

                    ABBOT
          Uh...go ahead.

                    MONICA
          We were friends in high school.

                    ABBOT
          Yes friends.

Paul and William step up and start talking to Troy. Monica
motions to Nicole to step off to the side so they can have a
private conversation.

NICOLE
More than friends, right?

MONICA
(smiling)
Yes much more. We dated for two years, and I dumped him because I didn't think he had much of a future. He was devastated.

NICOLE
Well you missed the boat on that one.

MONICA
Trust me, I have already beaten myself up over that decision. But he saw me here and we started talking. He said he could never stop thinking about me. Even after all these years, the old feelings started rushing back again...for both of us. We are going to dinner after this.

Nicole gives her a hug.

NICOLE
I'm so excited for you.

MONICA
Keep your fingers crossed. I think I've been given a second chance.

Cliff walks over and stands by Troy.

CLIFF
Listen up. Listen up.

No one pays attention and continues on their conversation. He looks over at Coach Griffin and mouths "help". Coach Griffin pulls out a whistle and blows two loud quick tweets.

COACH GRIFFIN
Can everyone please give your attention to Mr. Dunn?

Everyone immediately stops what they are doing and looks at Cliff.

CLIFF
Wow. I need to get me one of those.

Cliff takes a deep breath.

                    CLIFF (CONT'D)
               Mrs. Ferguson could you please come
               up here?

Ruby Rae Ferguson walks up and stands next to Cliff and begins
signing what Cliff is saying as everyone eagerly looks on.

                    CLIFF (CONT'D)
               After hearing about the fiscal plight
               of the Smith School, my partners and
               I raised 2 million dollars and bought
               the school from the bank and paid
               off all of its creditors. So as of
               10:30 last Friday morning the Smith
               School of the Deaf is completely
               debt free and under the management
               slash guidance of The Williams Walker
               Petree Hatcher and Dunn Law Firm.
               Which means the school will not be
               closing down! Not even close.

A huge roar erupts from everyone there. Ronnie, Abbot and
Monica are standing over to the side cheering as well.

                    RONNIE
               Williams Walker who and what? That's
               Mr. Dunn's law firm? I thought his
               firm was called the Dunn Group.

                    ABBOT
               Naw. He made that part up too.

Ronnie starts laughing. The cheering starts to die down.

                    CLIFF
               We want to completely revitalize the
               school by updating many of the
               existing facilities and buying the
               things necessary to allow the school
               to run in a more efficient manner
               including building a state-of-the-
               art computer lab that will be the
               envy of all the public and private
               schools in the area.

The cheering starts again.

                    CLIFF (CONT'D)
               The first order of business is to
               change the name of the school. We
               want the name to be flashy.

Samuel fist pumps.

                         SAMUEL
          Yes!

                         CLIFF
          Something more modern that the kids
          could relate to and take pride in.
          And since my firm is made up of a
          bunch of old fogies and would totally
          mess it up, we have decided to let
          you guys, the kids, name it. It will
          be a contest. Come up with your most
          creative ideas and the one we choose
          will get 1 year free tuition!

Cheers erupt again mostly from the parents of the kids.

                         CLIFF (CONT'D)
          Once our ownership was finalized, we
          accepted the resignation and
          retirement of its current
          administrator, Mr. Jacobs. We
          immediately formed a search committee
          for his replacement, and after
          spending an exhaustive search of
          about 5 minutes via conference call
          last night we came up with the perfect
          candidate. Troy "The Gun" Dunn!

The entire room erupts with even greater enthusiasm.

                         CLIFF (CONT'D)
          If he will have it.

Every eye in the room looks over at Troy.

                         TROY
          I can't think of anything else I
          would want to do more!

The adults start cheering, and the kids start running around
the room screaming, chest bumping, and giving each other
high fives.

                         TROY (CONT'D)
          I would like to say something.

No one pays attention as the room is in pandemonium. Troy
looks over at Coach Griffin. He pulls out the whistle and
blows two loud quick tweets.

                         COACH GRIFFIN
          Can everyone please give your
          attention to Troy. I mean Mr. Dunn.

Everyone looks over at Troy.

                    TROY
          Nicole please come over here.

A gasp comes over the crowd. Nicole teary eyed walks over to Troy. He grabs both of her hands and looks her in the eyes.

                    TROY (CONT'D)
          Nicole, if there were ever two people
          destined to be together it is us. I
          am so sure you are the one God had
          in mind for me when Paul wrote in
          Ephesians "Husbands, love your wives,
          as Christ loved the church and gave
          himself up for her". Christ lived
          and died for the church, and I always
          thought I could never love anyone
          that much until I met you.

Troy drops to one knee. Squeaks and squalls can be heard from the ladies.

                    TROY (CONT'D)
          It would be my ultimate honor if you
          will spend the rest of your life
          with me as my wife. Nicole will you
          marry me?

Tears start streaming down Nicole's face.

                    NICOLE
          Yes I will!

Troy stands up and the two embrace as the room explodes as everyone rushes up to the couple.

TITLE CARD: 3 MONTHS LATER

INT. NFL DRAFT BALLROOM

Rowdy football fans from all over the country fill out a packed auditorium wearing their team's colors, hats and jerseys. The ESPN analysts Chris Berman, Jon Gruden and Mel Kiper Jr. are sitting behind a V-shaped desk on a platform above and behind the audience in the auditorium.

The announcement stage in front of the large crowd, outlined at the bottom by bright lights, showcases the player selections of the NFL teams. There are 5 giant projection screens lined side by side and placed at the back of the stage. Highlights of the players that are chosen are shown on these screens as well as brilliant flashes of lights that burst randomly across expressing a spirit of festivity akin to a Fourth of July celebration.

                        CHRIS BERMAN (O.S.)
                    The much anticipated first pick of
                    the 2012 NFL draft is about to
                    transpire, and the room is buzzing
                    with conjectures on who the 49ers
                    will select.

                        JON GRUDEN (O.S.)
                    Sports fans all over San Francisco
                    are glued to their televisions right
                    now. This pick means a whole lot to
                    this franchise.

                        CHRIS BERMAN (O.S.)
                    I can tell you who else it means a
                    whole lot to. That's the five or six
                    players who think they are going to
                    be that pick and sport the red and
                    gold next year.

                        MEL KIPER JR. (O.S.)
                    Not only that Chris but the payday
                    for a first pick is gigantic. Last
                    year's first pick Cam Newton signed
                    a 4-year guaranteed $22,000,000
                    contract with the Carolina Panthers
                    with a $15,000,000 signing bonus and
                    this year's pick is predicted to
                    sign for even more.

                        CHRIS BERMAN
                    And here comes the commissioner.

ROGER GOODELL walks up to the podium.

                        ROGER GOODELL
                    With the first pick in the 2012 NFL
                    draft, the San Francisco 49ers select
                    Ronnie Pippen wide receiver Northern
                    California University.

A section of the event hall filled with 49er fans jump up
clapping and cheering. Grandma and Big Daddy, who are sitting
at a table with Ronnie, jump up as well throwing their hands
up in the air.

                        GRANDMA
                      (shouting)
                    Oh thank you Jesus!

Ronnie slowly stands up, and Big Daddy forcefully bear hugs
him.

                    RONNIE
               (smiling)
          Ok Big Daddy, I don't want the 49ers
          to place me on their injured reserve
          list before I even sign a contract.

                    BIG DADDY
          You did it man, you did it!

Ronnie walks his way through the auditorium around to the
side of the stage where he is shown by staff to enter a
hallway that takes him up to the podium. As he walks, he is
handed a 49ers hat and jersey. He puts on the hat and walks
to center stage and is met by Roger Goddell with a handshake
and a soft hug. They both hold up the jersey as cameras flash
all over the auditorium.

                    CHRIS BERMAN (O.S.)
          This might be a surprise to some but
          not to me. At 6 foot 3, running a
          4.2 with the softest hands in college
          football, I think this was a great
          pick for the 49ers. Is that fair to
          say Mel?

                    MEL KIPER JR. (O.S.)
          I think this was the **perfect** pick
          for San Francisco. They are filling
          a void that they desperately need.
          They have not had a receiver of this
          caliber since the days of, might I
          say, Terrell Owens.

                    JON GRUDEN (O.S.)
          Whoooa Mel! That's some big shoes to
          fill!

                    MEL KIPER JR. (O.S.)
          And Ronnie Pippen has all the tools
          with his size, speed, and hands to
          fill those shoes.

                    CHRIS BERMAN (O.S.)
          Agreed.

                    JON GRUDEN (O.S.)
          He's a good character kid too. Nothing
          but outstanding reports on what kind
          of person Pippin is off the field.
          When teams look at throwing millions
          of dollars at a rookie right out of
          college, I'm telling you character
          does matter.

                    CHRIS BERMAN (O.S.)
                The complete package. I can promise
                you the Bay Area is going to be
                rocking tonight!

EXT. VARIOUS STADIUMS

SERIES OF SHOTS-DIFFERENT DAYS

A montage of shots are shown of Ronnie playing for the 49ers
and making spectacular plays.

Alex Smith is in the shotgun. He gets the snap, and hits
Ronnie running a post pattern for a 60 yard touchdown.

Alex Smith is under center, gets the snap, and fires a bullet
to Ronnie as he jumps and catches the ball for 20 yards right
on the sidelines for a touchdown.

Alex Smith is in the shotgun. He gets the snap and passes to
Ronnie who is sprinting across the middle of the end zone
for a 15 yard touchdown.

Alex Smith is under center and gets the snap. Ronnie runs an
out and up. Alex pump fakes on the out and floats a 50 yard
bomb which Ronnie runs under, catches, and sprints to the
end zone.

INT. DUNN HOUSE

Troy, Nicole, Rebecca, Cliff, and a group of the kids dressed
in 49ers gear are cheering for Ronnie as he makes a catch.

INT. GRANDMA'S HOUSE

A back close-up view shows the old RCA television broadcasting
a 49ers game with Ronnie making an easy catch in the end
zone for a touchdown.

                    GRANDMA (O.S.)
                That's my baby!

The camera pans back to reveal the RCA television enclosed
in an enormous Habersham entertainment cabinet surrounded by
a Wisdom Audio's Infinite Wisdom Grand stereo system with
its 13-foot speakers. The camera continues to pan back
revealing a beautiful entertainment room with the 49ers'logo
embedded in a glistening marble floor. Big Daddy is seen
sitting on a Lexington Upholstery Salon sofa and Grandma is
sitting in a Sam Maloof rocking chair. It continues to pan
back through the ceiling revealing a rather impressive ritzy
estate with a football shaped swimming pool located on four
acres of gorgeous terrain on the California coast.

THE END

ABOUT THE AUTHOR

Timothy Sharer is the founder of Sharer McKinley Group.LLC and has been a financial advisor since 1993. He has mentored high school and college students for over 25 years as a layman in Sagemont Church's student ministry and is the current varsity basketball coach at Bay Area Christian School in League City, Texas. The loves of his life are his wife Debbie, daughters Jessica and Katelyn, mother Carolyn. and his three grandchildren Caden, Beckham, and Kambrey. His hero, of course, is his late father Richard "Skip" Sharer.

Made in the USA
Monee, IL
26 February 2020